Strange Tales

Strange Tales

John Reinhard Dizon

Published 2015 by Creativia

Book design by Creativia (www.creativia.org)

Cover art by http://www.thecovercollection.com/

Chapter One

The Lady on the Hill

Years before the peace negotiations were ever initiated in Northern Ireland at the turn of the century, there was a killing field where neither side ever claimed responsibility for a murder. It was at the foot of a hill known as the Devil's Drop, a place along the border of the Republic of Ireland not far from the Irish Sea. The bodies found at this site had been so horribly mutilated that none risked any association with such heinous crimes. Both the Royal Ulster Constabulary and the Garda Siochana patrolled the area regularly, eager to capture the monsters who would commit such crimes. The Irish Republican Army and the Ulster Defense Association placed bounties on the heads of the perpetrators, eager to distance themselves from such revolting brutality.

The citizens of the nearby city of Dundalk avoided the area like the plague, believing the place to be haunted by demons. Though the city was considered to be the birthplace of the mythical warrior Cu Chulainn, the Devil's Drop was said to be a place forsaken by the gods. At first they believed that it was the killers of the extremist groups that had committed the atrocities. When the activists vehemently denied these things, they next assumed it was the work of the authorities who sought to blame it on the dissidents. When the police and the military pledged to bring the murderers to justice, they realized it was the work of a demon that could not be thwarted by mortal means. Their only hope was to pray that God would intercede and banish this evil from their land.

The latest incident was determined to have occurred near the Northern Ireland border where signs of a struggle were discovered by Garda investigators.

The bloodstains appeared to have been two weeks old, indicating that the victim had been taken elsewhere before being butchered by her killer. The body had been found at the bottom of Devil's Drop, mutilated in a way detectives said was too horrible to describe. Even more terrible was the fact that forensics determined the victim was alive throughout most of the undertaking.

Garda Detective Siobhan Manley had been assigned to the case after the Irish President made a public statement vowing that the Republic would devote its full resources to the apprehension of the fiend. Both the Sinn Fein President and the County Louth representative in neighboring Ulster promised that the Constabulary would not rest until the monster was apprehended. The Irish Justice Minister assured the public that the citizens of Dundalk should feel safe and secure in their homes, though cautioning that isolated areas along the outskirts of town should be avoided until the psychopath was apprehended. Though Detective Manley's assignment had not been made a matter of public record, many of the residents along the Castletown River immediately took notice of the lovely young woman as she began her investigation.

She drove out to the bay area not far from Devil's Drop, deciding to rent a room and make it look like she was a student researching her thesis paper. She was a lovely girl with waist-length chestnut hair, dark blue eyes and a small upturned nose with pouting lips that most men found irresistible. It was only when they found out she was a cop did they keep their distance, and that was not the image she wanted to portray here in Dundalk. She needed all the help she could get, and if the local fishermen though they could teach her a thing or two, so much the better.

She went into the general store that was one of a long row of shops aligned in a commercial area overlooking the riverfront. She was dressed in a denim jacket and jeans, wearing her hair loose so as to attract casual attention. More than one set of eyes had found her to be a pleasant sight, but it was the presence of yet another woman in the store that was stealing her thunder.

Women were the harshest judges amongst one another, and here was no exception. The other girl had black hair, pale skin and an hourglass figure, but hers was the kind of face that most would consider beautiful. There was a difference between sexy and gorgeous, and this lass was past the curve. Her arched eyebrows accentuated her violet eyes and patrician nose, and her thick lips were perfectly shaped. Men might have been dying to take Siobhan to bed, but this lady was the type they would want to play for keeps.

The men seemed to be watching her as if a prize peacock had wandered into the store. She could not look at an upper shelf without one or two asking if they could reach something for her. Siobhan's twinge of jealousy was replaced by amusement as they appeared as circus clowns stumbling over themselves to assist her in any way. One of them was able to refocus their attention on Siobhan, offering to help carry her bundle out to her car. As she left the store, she and the lady caught each other's eyes and nodded politely.

Siobhan would soon learn that this was the Lady on the Hill.

Siobhan rose early the next morning and took a walk along the riverside, sorting out her thoughts and deciding on a plan of action. She wore a pea coat and black jeans along with hiking boots today, pinning her hair up so as not to attract as much attention as the other day. She hoped her plans worked better than they had at the general store when she got outdone by the lady on the hill. Today she hoped she would be perceived as a girl gone fishing, perhaps pursuing a pastime handed down by her father or brothers as the case might be.

She carried a fishing pole and a tackle box with her, and had a vague idea of how to go about this. She considered the notion that if she appeared to be a helpless lass without a clue, she might have a fellow or two come by and try helping her out. It was more than likely they would be married men, the same type that came over to help her and the lady on the hill. She wouldn't have to worry about them trying to walk her back to her cabin or get invited inside. It would be more about casual conversation, the kind that would give her the clues she needed to piece together what this place was about.

Apparently the murderer was abducting people from the village and bringing them to the cliff, before or after he killed them according to his whim. Of his twenty-one victims, eight were children, two were faeries and the rest were women. He would not take on someone who could overpower him or offer resistance. There were never signs of struggle at or near the cliff, so apparently the murders were taking place elsewhere and the corpses dumped afterwards, or some of them were rendered unconscious before being brought there. The problem is that no one had ever seen anyone suspicious in the area at any time the murders were committed, so most likely it was someone well known around the village. Yet, by now, someone would have surely known who was capable of doing such a thing.

It would have been impossible to rule out the extremist gangs in the area. If it had been either the UDA (*Ulster Defense Association) or the IRA (*Irish

Republican Army), even if the locals knew who was committing the murders, they wouldn't have dared say a word. Both sides had committed a number of atrocities in this area throughout the history of the Troubles, and there was little that had been found at the foot of Devil's Drop that would have been beyond either of them.

What both groups were denying and condemning was the murders of the little girls and the women. Neither of them had any love for faeries though they were accepted as volunteers when the ranks were thinned by arrests or assassination. Scores of women had been murdered by the terrorists for what they called treason, and the killings were publicly announced as a warning to all those who would betray their organizations. It was obvious that none of the women had been murdered for political reasons. Plus, no one in their right mind would have condoned the depravity of the sexual mutilations in each case.

It would have made sense that possibly a rogue militant might be acting on his own in conducting the killings, which could well have caused his fellow terrorists to turn a blind eye to his misdeeds. These people were not only in a death struggle against one another, but had everything to fear from the police and the military. If one of them had gone astray or even suspected of doing so, to take him out would cost them an arms-bearing soldier. If he was captured, there was always the possibility of him turning supergrass (*informer). This might be the best angle for her to pursue and see where it would lead.

The biggest problem she could foresee is if it led across the border into Northern Ireland. She would be going out of her jurisdiction, and if they found out she was a Catholic, she might end up the exception to the rule as an example of what the UDA could do to informers. On the other hand, if the IRA decided it was an in-house problem, they could well take exception to an outsider trying to infiltrate their ranks in bringing one of their own to justice.

She decided to chill out and begin her little game, opening her tackle box and fumbling with her gear to see who she could bait. They had given her some nasty-looking critters to place on her hook, and she could see that as the biggest problem to overcome here. She did not want to be impaling these things on fishhooks, but if she couldn't make this work, onlookers would realize that she didn't really belong here and was out looking for something else besides fish.

"Should be a great day for fishing, eh?"

She looked up at her first bite of the day, beholding a tall, athletically built young man in his mid-twenties, his sleepy-eyed look giving him a sluggish look that belied his cunning. His longish face was offset by a strange 1930's haircut that made him appear as a stalk of asparagus, shorn tight around the years yet sprouted freely from the top of his head.

"Aye, my Da always said that the fish are like people in a sense, they like having their breakfast early before they go about the day," Siobhan continued having trouble with her bait.

"Here, let me help ye with that," he grinned as she gladly handed over her green highlander salmon fly, which he expertly baited with her European Night Crawler. "Y'don't come out here much, do ye?"

"No, not as much as I'd like," she admitted. "I used to come out now and again with my Da. After he passed, I come out and it brings back memories of the good times."

"I know the feeling," he nodded, then held out his hand. "I'm Leo Blake. I'm a fisherman by trade, y'might say. I get a good catch and barter with the people in town. Either they'll pay cash for a good one, or I can pay my tab at the local shops with 'em. I love it out here, I can't think of a finer way t'make a livin'."

"Lovely," she smiled, shaking his hand. "My name's Siobhan, pleased t'meet ye. I was thinkin' of workin' my way along the shore, see which areas come up with the best bites. Why, I'll betcha there's some good fishin' out by that big cliff over there. You know how animals are, findin' refuge around places like that. They probably let enough leftovers drift out so that the fish know there's good eatin' thereabouts."

"Spoken like a true landlubber," Blake chuckled, "no offense. People sometimes think that our finny friends are as clever as our furry ones, or the feathery ones. Fact is, they do things by instinct that can be amazin' at times, but that's all it is, an innate sense that makes 'em do wonderful things kinda mechanically. That's the way of nature, y'know."

"You put that very well," she said admirably. "I suppose I'd just like to fish out there just to admire the bluff. It's a pretty wonderful sight."

"Well, people say it's haunted, and not without cause," Blake grew quiet. "You know, with the Troubles being as they are, quite a few people have gotten hurt out there, and not necessarily from climbin' about, if y'catch my drift. They say the banshees can be heard out there at night, and y'get the kids goin' out there and sprayin' paint and such. All in all, it's not th' nicest place for a young lady to be."

"I knew a girl who they say disappeared out that way, and I was always wonderin' what became of her," Siobhan confided. "I've heard stories that people went missin' here in Dundalk, but that seems to be the way things are all across the border."

"And where're you from, if ye don't mind my askin'?"

"I'm from Dublin, comin' up on vacation. I guess you've lived here all your life, eh?"

"Aye, born an' raised."

"Y'seem like the kinda fella that could keep a secret," she ventured.

"Well, I suppose so," he mused. "I don't have what y'call many close friends, I kinda keep to meself. Y'know how it is spendin' th' day catchin' fish. An' I'm not much of the type for pubs, or sittin' around the stovepipe passin' th' craic."

"I was tryin' to find out more about what happened to th' friend of a friend. The lass' name was Sinead McNamara. She disappeared hereabouts over the past year, and th' police found her body just a couple o' months ago. Whoever did her in treated her badly, an' the family's tryin' t' find what's bein' done."

"Aye," Blake stroked his chin thoughtfully. "Now, I'll tell ye, I know of one fella who could be of help in such a matter. He's Joe Lynch, he's with the Royal Ulster Constabulary. Of course he's from the other side, but he comes through here now and again doin' investigations and the like. He's kind of a rough fella, but y'know that goes with th' territory. I can tell him that yertryin' to find out about what they're doin' about the poor lass, an' we can see what he knows, I suppose."

"I'd greatly appreciate that," she smiled gratefully.

"Well, I'll be runnin' along," Blake took his leave. "I'll tell Joe about ye if and when I see 'im. Is there a place he might go lookin' for ye?"

"Sure, I'll be over at the cabins near Toberona Road not far from the bridge," she replied.

"That'll be fine," Blake smiled. "Y'can leave a message for me at the general store if y'like, I'm always around. The fishin's real fine out by the bridge, y'picked a great spot. Better than out by that ol' cliff."

"Say, just one more thing. Y'know anything about that house up there on the hill? You'd think whoever lives up there might've seen or heard something," Siobhan surmised.

"Actually, a young lady moved into the house just a week ago," Blake revealed. "She's all alone up there with her dog, a little poodle. She came down with her jeep to buy some things a couple of times, and th' fellas at the general store were fallin' all over each other to help her out. Seems she's an artist of sorts and doesn't leave the house, doesn't even have a phone. Every once in a while the kids playing out that way see her out foolin' with her dog, but that's about it."

"Aye, I guess that's how she ended up takin' th' place," Siobhan nodded. "Th' killin's probably happened well before she went inquirin', and ye know the realtor wouldn't have said anything to kill the deal."

"You're probably right," Blake waved as he headed off. "Good fishin'."

Siobhan decided to spend an hour sipping the coffee she brought in her thermos to build her storyline, tossing her weighted line into the river. She knew that word spread like wildfire in these little shanty towns, and Leo Blake would be repeating their conversation word for word at the end of the day before a potbellied stove in the general store. She wouldn't mind touching bases with Joe Lynch, but would decide whether she would reveal herself to him after meeting him. The RUC weren't always the most cooperative folks around, particularly when their jurisdiction was in question. If this fellow started throwing his weight around, he would be seeing Siobhan's back in short order.

She would give Jack O'Callahan a call back in Dublin after she returned to the cabin for lunch. He was a fellow Inspector at the Clontarf Station of Dublin Metro in Raheny, and also happened to be an ex-lover with who she had never completely gotten over. She knew the feeling was mutual, as he seemed to take particular interest in her out-of-town assignments and kept close tabs on her progress. They worked as partners from time to time, and Superintendent Mulcahy made Jack her liaison on this assignment as she called in her daily reports.

The problem with Jack, as far as she was concerned, was his over-protectiveness. He was a handsome fellow at 6'2", 200 pounds, with wavy chestnut hair and piercing blue eyes, and a confident swagger that came from his years as an all-star rugby player at the University of Dublin. He was the stereotypical macho man who wanted his wife taking care of the home and bringing up his kids. He insisted that she be the one to give up her job, when she couldn't fathom why he wouldn't to hang it up, especially since they were on the same pay scale. She loved her job and the sense of fulfillment that came with it. He didn't seem to cherish his own position nearly as much, but it was that old-fashioned male pride that would not allow her to be the breadwinner. It grew to such a point of contention that he ended up moving out on her.

She would not fool herself into believing she was the victim here. Much of her own stubbornness grew from the fact that she had been an only child, and her Da had placed all his hopes and dreams on his daughter. He was filled with joy as she worked her way through the University where she met Jack, only he had passed away a couple of years after her Mum, just a year before Siobhan graduated. She resolved to become a cop, succeeding where he failed due to a weak heart. It was as if she was overcoming vicariously in his stead, and she was not about to let this go at the pinnacle of her success.

She finally caught a small trout, and felt so sorry for him that she cut the fishhook loose as best she could and tossed him back into the sea. She always wondered what it would be like on the day of reckoning when she pulled her Walther P99 on someone. She knew that Jack had killed a perpetrator during a bank robbery years ago, and he was haunted by the memory ever since. It was one reason why he fell out of love with the job. Siobhan doubted she would experience the same kind of trauma, for anyone who pulled a gun on a woman would most likely have no consideration for either children or the elderly if challenged. She would not gamble her life on a chance that such a person would survive to hurt or kill others.

"Inspector O'Callahan, please."

"One moment."

She had returned to her rental cabin with no fish and without lunch, and decided to call in before returning to town for a bit to eat.

"O.C.," he sounded bored as usual.

"Hey, handsome, how's it hanging?"

"Same old stuff, lady. Got anything?"

"You don't sound like you're having a good day."

"About as good as a fellow can get with his ex over her head in hot water."

"Hey, simmer down, I'm doing just fine," she insisted, touched by the fact he was so worried about her. I made a contact with a local fisherman, and he turned me on to a local cop. See if you can look up a Joe Lynch with the RUC, probably working out of South Armagh."

"Will that be all, Inspector?" he was sarcastic.

"Hell, I've only been on the case for a day or so," she tried to get her Irish up towards him. "See here, there's a lady living on top of that hill where Devil's

Drop is located. See what you can find on her. I think she just bought or leased the property about a month ago. I don't think she'll be much of a lead, but we might as well take a look."

"Get a name on your fisherman? Might as well look at him too."

"Leo Blake," she replied. "It can wait until tomorrow, I'm gonna lie low today. Blake saw me fighting with my bait, so word'll get out that I don't know my arse from my elbow about fishing. Plus I'm gonna go back to town for some fish and chips, so they'll figure I'm done in for the day. Tomorrow I'll call to see what you've come up with, then I'll go out and see if I can find Joe Lynch."

"You know, this was a crappy assignment for you to have taken," Jack fumed. "This is an ongoing murder investigation, and you're way out of your jurisdiction. Plus you're in the middle of a war zone between the IRA and the UDA. They're not gonna like the idea of a woman sticking her nose around out there, and if they find out you're a cop, even the RUC and the Garda aren't gonna like the look of you."

"I'm not gonna let 'em know I'm a cop, silly," Siobhan insisted. "My story is that I'm out here channeling the good times with my Da. If I get chummy with anyone I'll tell 'em I'm up here on vacation from Dublin. I already told him I was curious about what happened to a friend of a friend a while back, and that'll be Sinead McNamara. If I come across Joe Lynch I'll tell him the same thing. My line'll be that I was coming up here anyway and told the relatives I'd ask around. It's seamless, Jack, I'm sure of it, don't worry."

"Like I told you, if you come across any heat, you need to step aside and let the big boys handle it," Jack began to go into his alpha male mode. "Nobody's gonna look crooked if you step aside for the hardcases. Those extremists don't feck around out there, everybody knows that. They'd just as soon bump you off and make an example of you than cut you slack because you're a woman. As a matter of fact, it'd probably work better for them to show they make no exceptions."

"You're scaring me shiteless, Jack," she teased him. "Look, I'm just doing what Mike Mulchay asked me to do. I'm digging up some leads, firming them up, and then I'll hand 'em over just as we agreed. I'm not planning to get in the middle of some sectarian gang war, that I can assure you."

"Okay, lass," he relented. "Just keep in touch. If anything at all comes up, you call my mobile phone number. Don't forget, if anything hits the fan I'm only a couple hours' drive away from you."

"I love you too, Jack."

"Yeah, talk to you later," he hung up.

She checked under her mattress for her gun and badge before heading out, locking up the cozy little cabin and slipping into her Kia Mini for the ride to town. She saw a couple of fish and chips places during yesterday's trip that would make up for the poor little trout that got away.

She had not the slightest indication that this would become the most frightful day of her life.

Chapter Two

Siobhan drove up to O'Keefe's Pub and Restaurant where they were selling fish and chips at a good price. She bought two orders to go, thinking she could do the extra one up later that evening in the microwave in case she got hungry. The place was set up in a split-level building with the restaurant in the rear and the pub area in front. It was designed so that the food buyers could come in through a rear door so as not to be going in and out through the drinking area. Siobhan was just about to leave when a short, pudgy man appeared in the adjoining entranceway to the pub.

"Excuse me, miss," she smiled cautiously, "May I have a word?"

"Well, sure," she stepped towards him, studying his weathered features highlighted by a receding hairline, beady eyes staring through wire-rimmed glasses, and a drooping chin. He beckoned her towards a table by the door which was in plain sight of everyone so that she would feel secure.

"My name's Joe Lynch," he introduced himself. He wore a red plaid jacket, gray corduroys and tan hunting boots, looking very much like one of the locals out for a day along the lake. "I'd heard from Leo Blake that you were here in town trying to get some information about one of the victims near Devil's Drop."

"Oh, is that what they call it?" Siobhan acted as if disconcerted by the name.

"Leo said he mentioned some of its history," Joe studied her face with the eye for detail of a veteran cop. She was fairly certain that he would not make her as a cop, at least not this time around. Despite what Jack thought, her little-girl charm was her biggest asset in this business. "I will tell you this, it's not the safest place to go looking about at this particular point in time. Now, I might be able to help you to meet up with some fellows that know the area and have come across some peculiarities. Keep in mind that the Garda and the Constabulary have strenuously pursued every lead we've gotten, but you just can't keep barking up every single tree, as one can imagine."

"Well, what kinda leads are they?" she wondered, going back into her Irish brogue. "I wouldn't want t'gobarkin' up th' wrong tree either."

"There's a place out in the woods not far from the hill where most of the incidents were reported," Lynch replied. "Some of the locals set out rabbit traps out thataways from time to time. It's a pretty restive place, not one that teenagers in love would've avoided while walking hand-in-hand, if you know what I mean. Plus lots of people just like walking through there to be alone with their thoughts, as it were. Yet this is how we see it through our eyes, those of us who have lived here all our lives. Someone like me—and those who've taken an interest in these incidents—wonder how it appears to an outsider. We wonder what your take on it might be, or what you think your friend's first impression might have been."

"Aye, an' t'see whether there would've been an apprehension about bein' in such a place, or on th' other hand, gettin' comfy an' lettin' one's guard down," Siobhan mused.

"Precisely," Joe replied. He was one of those who had a way of gritting his teeth while lowering his bottom lip, like more than a few elderly nuns she remembered from grade school. "Y'see, no one's ever got a grip on what they call this fella's *modus operandi*. Sometimes there's signs of struggle, while more often not. On some occasions it seems as if evidence is left behind, almost accidentally on purpose. Plus, with all the violence about stemming from the Troubles, one has to wonder whether or not the extremists are going about taking advantage of this fellow's evildoings and making their work seem like his."

"And I'm of a like mind myself," she replied. "I think the family and friends would find closure in knowing whether she was killed by militants or some serial killer. It wouldn't soften th' blow in any way, but at least they'd know who did it and why."

"Tell you what," Joe decided. "If you'd like to set here and have your chips, I'll make some calls and see if I can have a couple of fellows meet you out by there and walk you about. It's nice and Bridgman out, and there's only a single canopy of tree covering out there. Sometimes the sunlight makes it seem like one's in a tropical park of sorts. Having company out there'll make the trip less worrisome, considering the nature of the visit."

"Oh, I truly agree, sir," she smiled sweetly. Joe excused himself as he headed for the phone booth, and Siobhan took his advice and dug into her bag of fish and chips.

She considered the fact that Lynch was somewhat of a border-jumper, obviously spending as much time in these parts as he did. She knew that there were more than a few RUC officers who provided information to the UDA and were, in fact, members of the group. He could be passing along intelligence as to how the investigation was faring on this side and who was asking what kind of questions. This could be risky, but considering it was broad daylight and Joe's information was readily available to Jack and the Garda, she decided to take a look.

She almost felt like going back to her cabin and getting her gun and badge, but it would have been taking a chance on them getting suspicious. She had been leaving her purse in the Kia since she got here, and carrying it around at this juncture on a walk through the woods would have seemed as if she was bringing something extra along. Plus if she did get waylaid, whoever took her down would be holding a gun on her next, and she couldn't get loose and expect to outrun a bullet. And, if they found a badge on her, they might panic and make a desperate attempt to cover their tracks.

The thought of calling Jack crossed her mind, but that would most certainly have led to him calling the cavalry in. He would have the entire area crawling with undercover cops, and if the killer was lurking about, he would most certainly be no longer. She had a suspicion that Lynch held a key to the mystery, and for some reason he wanted an outside party to come across information that he had yet to act upon. There was just too much on the line for her to play it cautious. She had to follow this up before Lynch or someone else had the chance to find out who she really was.

"Okay, lass," Lynch returned to the table just as she had finished off a couple of pieces of fried trout. "The fellows'll meet you down by the foot of the Toberona Bridge in about fifteen minutes. They don't live far from there, so they'll just walk over. They're a couple of lads with dark hair, in their thirties, wearing plaid jackets just like mine. Just drive on up and tell them Joe sent you, and they'll show you where to park and walk you around."

"Sounds good, thanks, Joe," Siobhan wadded up the bag of fish and chips, tossing them in the wastebasket on the way out the door. She was a light eater, and the greasy food was more than enough for her at this time of day. She headed out and hopped into the Kia, gunning the engine and pulling out westward towards the bridge.

Once again she considered the notion of making a quick detour and grabbing her gun and badge, but again she figured they would be a liability if something did go sideways. She was a good athlete and a swift runner that even Jack O'Callahan had trouble keeping up with. If she got ambushed by militants along with these fellows, hopefully they would be able to create enough of a diversion for her to haul her arse back to the Kia to summon help. Plus, both Lynch and most likely Leo Blake knew she had come out here, so they would be calling somebody if she failed to reappear.

When she got to the bridge, she spotted two men standing along the staircase leading to the walkway to the bridge. They wore dark plaid jackets and jeans, along with heavy construction boots. She introduced herself and they told her to park off the side of the road near a clearing so as to avoid notice by the Garda who came around now and again looking for suspicious vehicles.

"The way things are hereabouts, y'never know what they consider suspicious," the tall man grinned.

She parked the car and came over to shake hands with the tall man, who was Robert, and the husky man who was Nathan. She introduced herself and they exchanged pleasantries about the weather before the men told her what they had planned.

"See there, you've got that trail leadin' under the bridge, and it goes on to that little secluded area that continues on towards the hillside," Robert pointed in the direction of the woodland past the bridge. Of course, you've got that dirt road that goes up the hill where that little house is, and beneath that is where those kids hang out and make all that noise at night."

"Do they really get a lot of kids down there?" she was surprised.

"Aye, an' they bring their packs of beer and boom boxes and raise all kinds of hell," Nathan replied. "They get away with it until th' Garda gets fed up an' brings the paddy wagon around, then ye don't see 'em for weeks at a time. Seems they get a kick outta hangin' out where all those people were rumored t'have gone missin'. Of course, the locals think it's pretty disrespectful. Nobody seems t'mind people walkin' about durin' th' daytime, though, so there'd be no harm in us showin' ye around."

"Sure, an' I'd appreciate it," Siobhan agreed. "A friend of mine was one of those who got lost around here. I'd like t'be able to go back an' tell th' family that at least I got to see th' place."

"An' y'can take our condolences back with ye when y'do so," Robert was emphatic. "Dundalk is a beautiful little city, an' what some do is no reflection on th' rest of us. We're all God-fearin' church-goin' folk who live clean lives an' want all our neighbors to know it."

Encouraged by his resolve, Siobhan followed them as they made their way down the narrow dirt road trailing beneath the bridge. It was about 11 AM and the area seemed fairly well deserted, save for the occasional vehicle driving over from Dundalk. She breathed in the scent of the river as they grew closer to the shoreline, with birds flitting about from the trees to the bushes. It hardly seemed possible that such atrocities could have occurred in such a restive place as this.

"See, right there's some mighty fine fishin', there under th' bridge," Nathan pointed out as they reached the grassy area at the foot of the trail. "Now, some folks say it depends on what kinda bait an' lure you're carryin', but it's a fact that tinkers'll come out here with nothin' but a string, a hook an' a worm, an' catch themselves a fine breakfast whenever they like."

"Aye, an' y'know what lyin' bastards they are, especially those that come from over th'border," Robert growled, beckoning her to follow as he started up another beaten path leading up to a knoll in the direction of the hill across from the treeline. "If they stayed on their own side, there wouldn't be a bit o'trouble anywhere to be found."

"What makes 'em liars?" she asked, feeling somewhat uncomfortable with the rude word. She glanced around to get her bearings, and it seemed that they would be on the high ground overlooking the field though the sloping area obscured the area from the bridge.

"Well, bein' Prods as they are," Nathan extended his arm, stepping aside so she could follow Robert up the hill. "Watch yer step, love. I'll be right behind ye in case you take a tumble. Sometimes you can slip and fall straightaways, an' I speak from experience."

Siobhan clambered up the steep pathway, the silence of the meadow broken only by the scraping of their boots seeking footholds. She considered the fact that they would have a commanding view of the hill, and they might even get a glimpse of the lady on the hill should she be going to or fro around this time before lunch. She wondered how many of the local fellows might come up this way to spy on her and find out what she did up that hill all by herself with her little dog.

"Y'know, those kids who come out here'll get blootered, listen to that rock music of theirs, an' have nightlong orgies," Robert grunted as they came closer to the top of the path. "It's th' little Proddy bastards, t'be sure. Sittin' out there, getting' stoned out of their minds on whatever drugs they carry, an' just screwin' their brains out. Of course, ye can't say this isn't exactly a bad place for screwin', as nice and peaceful as it is. A great view, ain't it, Nate?"

Suddenly her female instinct kicked in, and she stopped short to look around.

"It's an absolutely fantastic view from where I'm standin', fella," Nathan chuckled. She turned around and found Nathan just behind her on the slope so that his head was about a foot away from her loins, staring directly into her crotch.

"Well, fellas, I think I've had enough climbin' for one day," she decided. "I'm goin' back t'town and catch up on some chores. I sure do appreciate your time and effort showin' me around."

"Now, not so fast, lass, ye haven't seen anything yet," Robert exclaimed. "We've only got a bit to go, an' ye'll be in the best spot in th' whole area."

"Watch out now, missy, yerlosin' yer balance," Nathan reached out to grab both sides of her hips.

"Why, you stupid..." Siobhan cocked her fist, just as a hammerblow to the back of the skull nearly knocked her unconscious, causing her to swoon backwards.

"Okay, let's get her up there," Nathan grabbed her legs. Robert squatted down behind her and hooked his arms underneath hers as they lifted her up and carried her to the top of the knoll. She tried to struggle but could only see through a groggy haze as they laid her down inside a grassy hollow at the top of the hill. She could see one of them producing a length of rope, and she could feel her arms and legs being bound.

"C'mon, now, girl, let's get this party rollin'," Nathan cackled, rolling onto her tummy before forcing her legs up and pulling her backward into a squatting position. She could feel him tying her wrists behind her back so that it restricted her breathing and painfully distended her shoulder blades.

"Okay, girl, now yer gonna take communion today," Robert had exposed himself, holding a thick piece of branch in his hand. "We'll just put this in yer mouth so ye can't make a whole lot of noise an' disturb the peace."

He grabbed her by the hair and forced the branch into her mouth, all the way towards her molars. She recovered enough to fight back but at once was nearly knocked out by a right cross to the jaw.

"She givin' you trouble up front there, Robert?" Nathan huffed, tethering her ankles so she could not extend them past shoulder's length.

"Hell, you know they all get settled down after a while," Robert chuckled.

Siobhan could barely focus on where she was as the second blow had nearly knocked her out. She felt them tearing at her clothes but could do nothing to stop them, and could only hope to regain her senses long enough to try breaking free again. It would take everything she had to refrain from struggling before Robert could get another shot in.

Time seemed to drag on, and suddenly she had an inkling of what Hell was like, being in a place of eternal torment that went on forever and ever. She had no way of stopping these devils from tormenting her, and no way of knowing if or when it would ever end. She would do her best to fight back but she knew that she would receive another vicious blow for her efforts, and then the double assault would go on and on. She felt as if she was about to suffocate by the object in her mouth, and all she could do was keep her mouth open wide and her jaws relaxed so she could breathe as best she could...

"Well, I'll be damned. Will y'look at that."

"Ain't that something."

At once the attack was interrupted as the voices cut past the huffing and puffing of her torturers. She could feel them pulling away from her, and she gagged and spat until the stick fell out of her mouth.

"Now, c'mon, fellas, we're just up here mindin' our own business," Robert looked up at the four men surrounding the hollow. He reached for his clothes and was kicked in the face.

"It's well known that you Caddie bastards bring your whores up here an' rough 'em up, then lay th' blame on us," the leader snarled. "We're getting' heat from both sides o' th'border, an' we put out th' word. We told ye, an' we warned ye."

"Listen, fella, we don't want any trouble," Nathan pleaded before they stuck a gun in his face.

"You're already in over your head, boyo," another man growled.

"You got that right," Siobhan choked, spitting debris from her mouth. "I'm a cop. These bastards'll have hell to pay."

"Sure, and where's yer badge then, tramp? Is it in those whore clothes of yours?" a man pointed a gun barrel at her clothes strewn alongside the hollow.

"No, I didn't bring it with me, but all you got to do is…" she reached for her jacket, and one of the men's boots came down with force on her hand. She screamed with pain as she pulled it back, clenching it against her bosom, trying her best to avoid touching the naked bodies of her assailants.

"Look, if it's money yer lookin' for, we've got no problem with it," Robert tried to negotiate. "Just let us get downhill an' we'll take ye back t'my place, I've got…"

At once one of the men produced a .22 rifle, pointing it at Robert's face and pulling the trigger. The small bullet ripped its way between his eyes and left a large hole in the back of his head, causing his brains to spurt out over the grass behind him.

"Bejeezis!" Nathan cried. "Begorra, saints alive! Don't kill me, have mercy, I beg ye! I've got a wife an' kids, they'll have nothin' without me!"

"You lousy bastard, they've got nothing with you," Siobhan hissed at him.

"Ye got that right," the leader agreed, shooting Nathan in the face.

Siobhan did the best she could to maneuver herself away from the corpses. She looked up at them speechlessly as they silently assessed the situation at hand.

"Okay, listen, I'm with the Garda in Dublin," she told them. "I left my gun and badge behind just in case something like this happened."

"Listen, bitch, I'm not sure we should let ye live to tell the tale of what happened here," the leader insisted.

"You guys just saved my life," she exclaimed. "Why would I rat you out?"

"Didn't you just say you were a cop?" one of the men sniggered. She started to say something just before a boot smashed across her jaw and knocked her out cold.

She began coming to her senses gradually, without the remotest idea of where she was. She immediately began feeling around for her clothing and realized she had been covered with a dirty blanket. She was lying on a cold, hard surface, and began curling herself into a ball as she tried to regain her bearings.

"Looks like the whore's comin' around," she heard a voice cutting through the fog in her head. Her jaw was killing her, and her head was throbbing as if of the mother of all hangovers. Her bones were aching from the cold, and she figured she had been out for a few hours by now.

"Help…me…" she could hear her own voice as if coming out of a cone.

"Say there, bitch, we got a call a couple of hours ago that came like a reprieve from the Governor," one man chortled. "He asked us not to chop ye up until he could get a look at ye. I think all of us here could see why. You're not too bad-lookin' for a Croppie slut."

At once she could hear the sound of a garage door being automatically raised, and realized she had been taken away from the Toberona Bridge area. She had little choice but to pull the smelly blanket tight around her to protect herself as best she could.

"Shite," one of the men growled. "It's Joe Lynch."

"Now who in hell called that bugger down here," another man grunted. The area was dimly lit by what appeared to be emergency lamps, and she could discern the silhouettes of about six or seven men as they stood around the darkened garage. As the overhead door rolled to a halt, a big man standing about 6'2" and weighing about 210 pounds strode into the building. She could make out a thick head of gray hair, and piercing blue eyes that cut through the dark. At once she knew this was not the Joe Lynch who sent her to the bridge to her doom.

"Where is she?" the big man demanded. He was dressed in a dark gray suit and black Western-style boots.

"Right there," one of the men pointed to her as she managed to rise into a sitting position.

"Any of you touch her since she been here?"

"Hell no," a man replied. "We threw that blanket over her, and put up her clothes so she wouldn't run off."

"Aw reet," he replied, walking over and squatting down beside her. "Hear tell you said you was a cop."

"You're Joe Lynch, the real one," she croaked, her throat sore from the dirty objects forced into her mouth hours ago.

"I got a couple of calls from Dublin about some girl who might've got lost down here, fits your description," he replied quietly. "You know, you're a helluva long way from home. You're in pretty bad shape, and there's not a friend in sight."

"Look, help me out," she begged. "I'm a fellow officer. Don't leave me here like this."

"You should've thought about this when you first took this assignment," Lynch shook his head. "They've been cuttin' women to pieces out here. What made you think you were gonna be an exception?"

"I just came out here to get some leads," she explained hoarsely. "I wasn't expecting these bastards to set me up."

"We'd been watchin' those two buggers for a long time," Lynch explained. "We suspected they'd been bringing whores out there and roughing 'em up, then blamin' it on the UDA. If they went too far, or one of those biker gangs out there found the whores and did 'em in, then they'd blame it on the Devil's Drop killer. We figured they'd screw up sooner or later, and, well, when a good-lookin' lass like you came across their path, well, they couldn't resist tryin' it in broad daylight."

"Can I have my clothes back?" she began to weep.

"Joe?" he motioned, and one of the men came out of the shadows and threw her clothes on the ground beside her.

"So are they the killers?" she mumbled, grabbing her shirt and pulling it on as quick as she could. She would cover her nakedness and worry about her underwear later.

"Nah, they're a couple of scum-sucking bottom-feeders," Lynch smirked. "Street trash IRA wanna-bes. There's garbage like that on both sides of the border, takin' advantage of the Troubles to prey on innocent folk. We try an' keep our side under control as best we can. Unfortunately you an' yer friends in the Garda don't do as good a job as we do."

"None of can do as well alone as we can working together," she said softly.

"Yeah, well, go back and tell it to Mulcahy," he rose to his feet.

"How did you...?"

At once, a man came up behind her and plunged a needle into her shoulder. She winced and bucked, turning to push the hand away, but she was too beat up to react quickly enough. She desperately snatched her pants from the floor, shoving her feet into them, and she barely pulled them up over her bottom before she went out like a light.

Chapter Three

Jack O'Callahan arrived in Dundalk that next morning as a man possessed. The Garda found the Kia Mini at the foot of Toberona Bridge with all its windows smashed, all tires slashed, dents and scratches all over the car, and the trunk and hood pried open with the engine torn asunder. They brought out the bloodhounds but, away from the attack scene at the crest of the drumlin, there was no trace of Siobhan Manley to be found.

The Garda put out a red alert throughout the Dundalk region and the neighboring County Louth in Ulster, with a media campaign urging anyone who might have seen the missing detective to notify the police or Army immediately. Checkpoints had been set up within a 100-mile range, and posters and flyers with Siobhan's photo had been plastered all over the vicinity. Everyone Siobhan had been in contact with had been questioned, from the owner of the fishing cabins to the manager of the general store near Toberona Road. To a man, no one had a clue as to where she might have gone that morning before she disappeared.

Jack made contact with Joe Lynch and scheduled a meeting at O'Keefe's Pub that afternoon. Lynch seemed somewhat perturbed but maintained his professional decorum as he took a seat at a rear table in the pub with the Garda inspector.

"This is turning into the media event of the year hereabouts," Lynch noted as he sipped his tea. "As it should be, of course. Anyone who attacks a police officer doubtlessly would have no concern whatsoever in harming anyone else. This individual is a public menace who must be taken down at all costs."

"Well, I'll tell you," Jack stirred his own cup, staring at Lynch intently, "this particular officer happens to be my partner. I've been working with Manley for six years and I intend to find her, one way or the other. The last time I talked to her was yesterday morning, and she gave me your name as being referred by a Leo Blake. The obvious question is, who's Leo Blake?"

"Now that's a good question," Lynch replied. "There's lots of Joe Lynches in Ulster and the Republic, but I'll bet there's not as many Leo Blakes. Have you asked around?"

"Not yet. You're the first fellow I looked up. I wanted to find out whether I should be inviting Blake for tea, or have a squad car pick him up. I'm thinking I'll get a fix on him, and decide from there."

"I wouldn't mind hearing back from you about that. Sure, and it's no crime to be dropping a fellow's name, even if it happens to be a police officer, but there is a thin red line to be aware of. If he's pushing my name around to earn favor, or if someone else's doing something similar, that could be construed as impersonation."

"I'm just trying to get a handle on how you're remaining so active here south of the border," Jack wondered. "With the Troubles being what they are, it would stand to reason that those trying to bend the rules would feel like they had an ace in the hole with someone operating out of bounds."

"Well, let's put it this way," Lynch leaned his elbows on the table. "When stuff like this hits the fan, law enforcement agencies get real aggressive at first, but when they don't get immediate results, they turn defensive and anal-retentive. If your people don't find this girl in twenty-four hours, they'll go into cold case mode and start putting their confidential stickers all over the place. My people send guys like me over here to find out what your folks aren't willing to share with us."

"Okay, then, let's cut to the chase," Jack decided. "I'm here from Dublin. The Garda here in Dundalk isn't exactly jumping for joy over me coming in to lend a hand. I don't think they're any more excited about me being here than they would be about you. Why don't we join forces and see what we can find without the locals getting in on it?"

"I'd think the door should swing both ways," Lynch cocked an eyebrow. "If you were to come up with any information that would help my search, I'd expect you'd be willing to share and share alike."

"Your search?" Jack was puzzled.

"The problem we have here along the border is that whatever they can't solve, they arbitrarily blame on the powers-that-be in Northern Ireland," Lynch was brusque. "There is a sizeable population that believes that the Protestant community in Ulster is all for one and one for all. They fail to distinguish between law abiding citizens and the extremist organizations, much less our law enforcement agencies. If this officer is not found, the consensus will be that she got abducted by loyalist militants, which will mean that yet another murder sails right under the radar. I'm sure you're aware of the Devil Drop murders that have been taking place here for some time."

"As a matter of fact, I'll take you into my confidence by letting you know that Inspector Manley was here investigating those murders," Jack stared into his eyes, searching for a reaction which was not forthcoming. "She came down here on her own and I maintained phone contact. She hadn't been here for forty-eight hours before her disappearance. The last I heard from her, she gave me your name and Leo Blake's. She was briefed on the situation here, how the blame was being tossed back and forth between the UDA and IRA, as well as the RUC and the Garda. The Sinead McNamara murder pretty well sank it for our people in Dublin. It was a damned nasty piece of work and frankly, the higher-ups decided enough was enough. We plan to bring the bastard—or bastards—in, one way or the other. Siobhan was one of those who found it particularly distasteful, and jumped up and down waving her hand until she got picked."

"Let me assure you, Inspector, we have this crap going on right on our doorstep, and we've pretty well had our own fill of people pointing their fingers and saying we're turning a blind eye to it all," Lynch frowned. "I won't deny that politics plays a big part in what goes down here, but there is no one anywhere who would condone the butchery that's taken place around that hill. Now, I know as well as you that the UDA has hacked up plenty of people who've crossed their path, but they've always taken responsibility and gave reasons for what they've done. Same with the IRA, even though they're more prone to using bullets than knives and axes. Most law enforcement agencies I've talked to agree that these murders indicate that the killer seems to be savoring the experiences."

"That's why I don't think she got snatched by the militants," Jack insisted. "They would've asked for a ransom or made demands in exchange for her release. I've got a sick feeling that I'm in a race against time. I could use your help here, Lynch."

"Okay, so you've got my mobile number, let me get yours," Lynch agreed as Jack handed him a business card. "I think my first move is to look up this Leo

Blake fellow and see what he has to say about bandying my name about. I'd suggest you might want to take a look at that lady on the hill. She recently bought that house up there and has been keeping pretty much to herself. I'd say she's got a commanding view of the area and might have seen something that she might not have thought unusual at the time."

"Sounds like I'll be taking a trip up that hill," Jack nodded. "Let me know how things go with Leo Blake."

* * *

The house on the hill was a two-story frame building with ceramic tile that was ideal for weather conditions along the coast, protecting it from coastal storms and erosion from sea water. It had been recently painted, most likely before the lady bought the house. She had a small jeep parked out underneath a carport in back, adjacent to a shed that held supplies and housed an emergency generator. There was also a small garden which she apparently took time to cultivate quite nicely. At first glance she seemed to be a classy lady, and he had to wonder what the hell she was doing out here in an area such as this.

He knocked and waited for a while, hearing movement within and noticing the peephole in the solid wooden door. He was dressed in a gray suit with white shirt and designer tie, confident that he projected the image of the upwardly-mobile young professional. He smoothed his hair back as the door opened, and was nearly taken by surprise at the sight of the beautiful woman.

"Good morning, ma'am," he smiled, showing his badge. "I'm Inspector O'Callahan with the Garda in Dublin. We're investigating a missing persons case in the Dundalk area and I was hoping I could ask you some questions."

"Well, I suppose so," she said, stepping past him as she closed the door softly behind her. She wore a white blouse and a full-length black dress, her wavy black hair spilling over her shoulders onto her generous bosom. She detected the scent of lilac which was annoyingly arousing. "If you don't mind, my little dog is under the weather and I'm hoping he'll sleep off whatever is ailing him."

"Of course not," Jack agreed, stepping over to the paved walk surrounding the house and lining the garden area. "We're investigating the disappearance of a police officer, an Inspector Manley, Siobhan Manley. She rented a fishing cabin down by the river a couple of days ago. She had been conducting a routine investigation of her own and disappeared sometime yesterday afternoon."

Jack produced a photo, and the lady's eyes lit up.

"I do believe I saw her at the general store the day before," she replied. "You see, the fellows at the store can be flirtatious at times, and they do go out of their way to be helpful. I was doing my best to complete my shopping when I noticed another lady in the store who also caught their attention. If my memory serves correctly, I think it might have been her."

"Do you remember anything unusual, any conversations she might have had with anyone beside the cashier, any exchanges or altercations?"

"No, not at all," she recalled. "We smiled and nodded at one another as we passed, as neighbors do. To tell you the truth, I'm always quite content to finish my shopping and get on my way when I'm in town. People can be quite inquiring, and I'm somewhat of a private person myself."

"I imagine you've got plenty of privacy all the way up here," he glanced out at the breathtaking view of the Irish Sea bordered by the greenery of the shores of Dundalk. "Do you get any trespassers, people coming up here for directions, tinkers, anything of the sort?"

"No, not at all," she replied, her violet eyes alluring in the sunshine. "It would be quite a hike for one to come on foot, and anyone in a motorcar would be foolish to come up here when the shops on the riverfront are just nearby."

"You ever hear anything unusual down there, at the foot of the hill?" Jack nodded towards the clearing, at the end of which was the infamous drop about a hundred yards away from the house. "I don't come out after dark, living alone here by myself," she said pointedly.

"Glad to hear it, ma'am," Jack replied. "Well, I just thought I'd check, see if you heard or saw anything suspicious. Here's my card, if you do come across anything you think might help, please give me a call."

"I haven't been in town today, I do hope the young lady is okay."

"We intend to find her, ma'am," Jack was resolute. "Thanks for your cooperation. Have a nice day."

He hopped back into his late-model Bentley Flying Spur, gunning the engine and heading back down the hill. He decided to drive by the foot of the hill, at the bottom of Devil's Drop, to get a look at the killing field and say a prayer that Siobhan would never become part of its legend.

* * *

Joe Lynch had driven by the foot of the hill more than a couple of times and never failed to be incensed by the depravity of the area. The rock walls and ledges were covered with graffiti, and stones had been set in place so that druggies could conduct satanic rituals that were probably more of a creepy-crawling experience for most than an occult event. The area stunk like urine, and it made him sick that these losers would be doing such things in a place where so many people had been left to die.

He decided to pay a visit to the Dundalk Banshees Motorcycle Club along Toberona Road. The Banshees were one of the biggest biker crews in Dundalk, and though they were no more or less rambunctious than any other in Northern Ireland, they had been at loggerheads with the RUC on a regular basis. There were about five of them fiddling with their bikes out front, and there were no friendly faces in sight when he pulled up in his Fraser-Nash Le Mans.

"Say, fella, the sign says Members Only," one of the bikers called over.

"Well, whyn't you follow me inside and come throw me out?" Lynch shot back before shoving his way through the door.

He adjusted his vision to the darkness of the converted tavern, spotting a half dozen bikers and a couple of mamas lounging about the grungy clubhouse. Sitting on a huge overstuffed red leather armchair near the jukebox was Crusher Lisowski, the president of the club.

"Hey, I smell pork, it must be lunchtime," a hulking biker turned away from the pool game in progress by the far wall.

"It won't do you a damned bit of good with all your teeth kicked out," Lynch sneered at him. The biker, standing as tall as Lynch and outweighing him by twenty pounds, swaggered over as they eyeballed each other balefully.

"Whatever happened to 'protect and serve', Inspector?" the Crusher asked mildly as he puffed on a Cuban cigar.

"That's for law abiding, tax-paying citizens," Lynch came over as the big biker headed out the door, glaring at Joe as he walked past him. "Pay your taxes lately?"

"So are you collecting taxes these days, or lookin' for a kickback?" the Crusher studied his cigar.

"If I was, it'd be more than you could afford, I'd make sure of it," Lynch stood with his fists on hips. "I'm looking for a missing cop. Think you can help me?"

"Hey, Spike, any cops over there behind the table?" Crusher called over before getting up and looking down at his armchair. "Nah, don't see any cops here."

"Listen, clown, you know who I'm talking about, that one they're busting balls over from up in Dublin," Lynch growled. "The Garda's all over the place, and if that's not good for me it's definitely no good for you."

"Okay, okay, we're on the lookout," Crusher set his hands around make-believe binoculars and peeked up at Lynch. "See ye in th' funny papers."

Lynch took his leave, satisfied that he had covered his tracks with the Garda and on the street between O'Callahan and the Banshees. He only hoped that the UDA volunteers he had left Siobhan Manley with had done likewise.

A couple of hours later, Jack O'Callahan's Bentley was pulling up alongside a small shack along the outskirts of Dundalk past the riverfront area. He had done some checking and found out that Leo Blake lived out this way. He was told that Leo had been in town at the break of dawn as he was wont to do, and would either be out by the river or at the house, depending on his luck at casting his line that morning. He pulled up on the grass alongside the weather-beaten shack, trudging along the sandy grass to the front door where he knocked and waited.

"Top o' th' mornin'," the man opened the door to greet Jack. "How can I help ye?"

"Mr. Blake? I'm Inspector O'Callahan, I'm on a missing persons assignment and I wanted to ask you some questions. I'd been doing some inquiring about town and found that you'd spoken with Siobhan Manley, the Garda inspector that went missing yesterday."

"Uh-*huh*," the man nodded, stepping out onto the rickety front porch, leaving the door ajar as he came out alongside Jack. "Well, now, ye know that we get our fair share of tourists down this way, an' I can't say I'm not the type who goes out their way to help out. I'm whatcha'd call a fish monger myself, an' I make my way by hobnobbin' with folks. I don't have a TV as I make do with my radio, but down at the store there was talk that th' lass who'd been out and about a day or so ago might've gone missin'."

"She called me shortly after she spoke to you, and said you mentioned an Inspector Joe Lynch during your conversation."

"Aye, then that must've been her," he gritted his teeth, lowering his bottom lip as some folks did when contemplating something or other. "She'd asked about the goings-on out by that cliff near the bridge, an' I told 'er that Joe might be the best one t'ask about such things. He's with th' police, y'know, an' if anyone knew anything, it'd be he."

"I take it you hadn't seen her since yesterday morning," Jack surmised.

"Nay, an' if I had, I sure would've mentioned it t'someone if they'd asked. Of course, I wasn't quite sure that she was the one they were talkin' about. I saw th' posters an' flyers an' heard the craic, but y'never think that somethin' like that'd happen to one that y'just got done speakin' to."

"Here's my number," Jack gave him a business card. "If you hear or see anything give me a call. She went missing right there around the bridge area not far from the hill out that way. They found her car trashed out there this morning. If you find anything on the beach she might have dropped, or see anything that looks like it might have been caused during a scuffle—*anything*—let me know, okay?"

"Sure will," he replied. "I certainly hope she turns up an' everything's okay. She sure seemed like a sweet young lass."

"Thank you, sir. Have a great day."

He watched as Jack got back into his car and drove off, then headed back into the house and locked the door behind him. He set the business card down on the antique radio by the window near the wall before shuffling off to the rear bedroom.

"Who was that?" Siobhan Manley asked, lying on the cot in the tiny room. She had been given strychnine shortly after she recovered from the sedative she was injected with at the UDA safe house in South Armagh. She had been driven back to Dundalk, and the strychnine gave her severe stomach cramps so that she had been barely able to move, much less walk.

"Ah, just some tinker," the man she knew as Joe Lynch replied, staring at her through his cheap wire-rimmed glasses. "I sent him away. Not to worry, I sent a friend into town to make sure those UDA killers and that fellow impersonating me around town aren't still lookin' for ye. Once the coast is clear, we'll send for the Garda an' get all this sorted out."

She wanted to continue her argument that he needed to leave her here and call the police anyway, but he was adamant that the UDA was scouring the streets looking for her. She was too sick and in too much pain to piece together the whys and wherefores, and could only reach for the glass of milk on the nightstand that brought her blessed relief. She took as big a sip as she could stand, and within minutes she was back in dreamland, dead to the world.

Chapter Four

The bodies of Michael Dolan and Patrick Byrne were found at the bottom of Devil's Drop the next morning, and a notice was sent to the RUC by the UDA in County Louth taking responsibility for the murders. It was indicated that the two men were noted IRA sympathizers who had committed crimes against the people of Ulster, but would not specify exactly what those crimes consisted of. The story spread like wildfire, and it had a side effect of crowding the search for Siobhan Manley out of the headlines.

Inspector Joe Lynch was irate as he stormed into the social club in the Bessbrook section of South Armagh that was run by the UDA. The enforcers at the door made little attempt to stop him as he stalked past the customers at the bar and headed straight for the back office where UDA commander Bill Staunton sat perusing the morning paper.

"So is that what you call good press, Bill?" Joe growled, closing the door behind him. "You think you've struck a blow for law and order with that flash of inspiration?"

"What the hell were y'thinkin' we were gonna do with two dead bodies, leave 'em up there so they could tie 'em in with th' missin' cop?" Bill stared at him. He was a barrel-chested red-haired man with a thick goatee and piercing green eyes. "We should've just finished her off with those two Taigs (*Catholics), but we made the stupid mistake of bringin' her back to the safe house. Sure, an' there would've been plenty 'o heat in th' kitchen, but it would've been far better than havin' these bastards turnin' the county inside out lookin' for her."

"You can't go around killing cops," Lynch slumped down in a seat before Staunton's desk in the small office. "This was a shitstorm waiting to happen. That bitch was going to get herself in hot water sooner or later snooping around here unannounced. She knows too much at this point, you're going to have to get rid of her. She already knows I've got connections to your people, and she saw your boys do those IRA wannabes in. You may have to put her down at this point, Bill."

"Well, I'll tell ye, that may be easier said than done at this point," Staunton rocked slightly in his swivel chair. "It seems we turned her over to some folks who may be doing some of that dirty work at the foot of that cliff."

"Folks?" Lynch stared at him. "What the hell are you talking about?"

"Don't get your britches twisted," Staunton scowled. "Y'know there's a lot of sick bastards who've developed an attachment for that damned area. Y've got druggies, devil worshipers, even the bikers go down there t'party now and again. Officially, both our people and the Croppies (*Catholics) are sayin' it's the work of the Devil's Drop Killer. In truth, we all know that we've all dumped the occasional corpse over the side and blamed it on the psycho. Then again, sometimes we just let some people fall into the wrong hands, shall we say."

"So who in hell did you turn that girl over to?"

"That's the tricky part," Staunton revealed. "Lots of times we'll just tie the person up, pull a burlap sack over them, and set them out on those rocks where the shitheads do their pagan rituals. We wait until someone comes along an' picks 'em up, an' then we'll be on our way afterwards."

"Have you gone out with them when they drop the victims off? How do you know the cops won't show up when you leave them out, especially someone like her?"

"Nah, I never go, but I make it my business to know who does. Plus, t'my understandin', there's a phone number they call first t'leave a message. Th' party on th' other end's very well organized. We have an answerin' services where they leave messages for us advisin' of regular changes of th' number. We tried checkin' ourselves one time and found that it was one of those free Internet phone numbers, an' it's always changin'. We kinda consider it our disposal service."

"Are ye feckin' blootered, man?" Lynch squinted at him. "How in hell do you know it's not the Devil's Drop Killer?"

"Let me ask ye, fella," Staunton smiled tautly. "When tryin' t' wash blood off yer hands, d'yefindyerselfhavin' a big problem over which brand of soap ye use?"

Jack O'Callahan heard the news that morning and went straight to the Garda Station at the Dundalk District Headquarters, not far from the Dundalk Railway Station off Ecco Road. There he met with Garda detectives who redirected him to the Homicide Squad, and they gave him all the information about the double homicide he needed to know.

Dolan and Byrne were IRA associates who had an unsavory reputation throughout the community and were considered low-lives even among the activist community. Both had relatives who held rank in the Official IRA, and they used their specious status as a cover for a number of scams and misdemeanor crimes. It got them a spotty reputation along the underworld and also helped them establish a considerable record with the Garda and the RUC. Among the militants, they were considered bottom-feeders and nearly escaped kneecapping by the Provos (*Provisional IRA) on more than one occasion.

Forensics determined that the victims' blood was an exact match for that found on the hillcrest where it was found that Siobhan had disappeared. Undoubtedly these two had been killed at or about the same time she was abducted. He had no doubt that whoever killed Dolan and Byrne had something to do with Siobhan being taken, and his best hope was finding out who knew who the killer or killers might have been.

Dolan and Byrne had also caught a pretty good beating a few months ago from the Dundalk Banshees Motorcycle Club for selling them some counterfeit insurance cards that had brought some big heat down on them from the Garda. Jack got hold of the police reports on the incident, made copies, then went on his way. He figured that someone involved in the incident had more than a passing acquaintance with these fellows and decided to find out a bit more.

Guillotine Gordon was the sergeant-at-arms of the Dundalk Banshees, and he lived near the Riverside Crescent not far from the downtown area. He invested considerable money in a Harley-Davidson that had been imported from Glasgow, and it was his pride and joy that he only allowed the club's mamas to service with care. His neighbors found it amusing that the bike appeared to cost twice as much as the ramshackle cottage he lived in.

He wheeled it out of his garage onto the driveway, then pulled a diaper out of his saddlebag and daubed it with car polish, checking for smudges. He decided that if it was smooth enough for a baby's arse, it should work for his chopper. He inspected it thoroughly before hopping on, gunning the motor and heading down the road towards the clubhouse. He thought of stopping by the pub on the way over, grabbing himself a pint and a six-pack to stuff in the cooler when he got there. It was a nice day, and he figured on taking one of the mamas for a ride and some cuddling out by the river afterwards.

He saw a vehicle pulling up from behind and tailgating him, and he cursed and swore as he pulled aside to give the Bentley enough room to pass by. Normally he would play the hardass and let the bastard suck on his tailpipe, but this fellow flew up out of nowhere and was obviously in a hurry. This sort of silly bugger would likely not know his arse from his elbow, and might try passing and sideswipe the bike instead. That would probably result in him having to beat the stuffing out of the dumbshite, and having to spend the day at the Garda station and send the bike to the shop was definitely not worth it.

Gordon reluctantly made room, and as they approached the bend, the driver pulled up parallel to him and signaled him to pull over. Guillotine was astonished as he was wearing his colors, and no one in their right minds would have played such foolishness with a biker, much less a Banshee. He flipped the driver off, and suddenly the bugger started accelerating before swerving as if to cut Gordon off. Guillotine began easing on his brakes, reluctant to stop short and risk going into a skid.

"Hey, you stupid son of a bitch!" Gordon roared, parking the Harley on the grassy side road and storming over to the Bentley. "You tryin' t'getyerself killed?"

"Garda," Jack O'Callahan hopped out of the car, holding his badge up in his right hand and his SIG Sauer P226 by his left hip. "Hands behind your head and turn around."

"Hold on, fella. How do I know that's a real badge?"

"There's one helluva way to find out, lad. I said turn around."

Gordon reluctantly did as he was told, and Jack drove his right knee into the back of Gordon's while grabbing his shoulder, forcing him to a kneeling position.

"Okay, boyo, here's the deal," Jack put the cuffs on him and prodded him back towards the Bentley. "I want to know everything about those two sons-of-bitches that got dumped off the Devil's Drop last night."

"Are ye feckin' kiddin'!" Gordon exclaimed. "I've got an alibi! I was at the club most o' th'night, an' when I left I was hardly in shape t'ride! Y'might get me ferridin' under th' influence, but damned if I had anythin' t'do with those two getting' offed!"

"You threw a pretty good beating on them a few months ago after they dumped those counterfeit insurance cards on you," Jack replied after herding Gordon into the Bentley and slamming the door behind him. He walked around to the driver's side and got in as he continued. "Maybe the UDA issued a statement claiming responsibility, but it didn't seem to have a whole lot of motive other than these two being rats that have been running loose for a long time. I think you have a lot more motive than that."

"Whoa, hold on, wait a second!" Gordon was taken aback. "You're trying to pin this on me, ye bastard, ye'd better bring me in so I can call my solicitor! Yer just fishin' for some way to close yer case, an' you're in the wrong pond, fella!"

"Okay, try this on," Jack reached over and grabbed him by his scraggly blond hair. "The Garda hasn't informed the media that their DNA was found at the scene where the missing inspector went missing the other day. I thought you'd like to be the first to know, since you're the one we're going to pin this on."

"What the feck are y'talkin' about!" Gordon was wild-eyed, straining against his cuffs. "I haven't seen either of th' bastards since we lit 'em up! You can work this anyway y'like an' it's not gonna fit, yer just wastin' yer time!"

"You see how this is going to go down," Jack released Gordon's hair as he explained patiently. "They're planning to release the information to the press as soon as we have a fall guy. We're going to have you sent to Maghaberry, and you'll be going in as a suspected cop killer since most of us assume that Inspector Manley is already dead. We're also going to pin the murders of Dolan and Byrne on you, so the Provos will be going after you on principle, and the RUC aren't about to lift a finger to help, since a cop killer on one side of the border is as bad as being on the other. Plus, I'll make sure they keep you there until the Provos get the job done."

"What the feck are you trying to do?" Gordon was frantic. "What is it you want from me!"

"A name," Jack replied. "The missing inspector is my partner, Siobhan Manley. She's also a personal friend and we're very close, if you know what I mean. I will not rest and I will do anything and everything I have to do to find her. I need to know the name of your RUC contact, the guy in your area your club calls when you get in a jam. You do me the favor and we'll both forget this conversation ever took place. I warn you, though, if you take off and give him a heads-up, I'll find you and do everything I said I was going to do, just for starters."

"All right, boyo," Gordon's face was flushed with anxiety, "You got a deal."

Within a short time, Jack O'Callahan found out everything he wanted to know.

It was late afternoon by the time Joe Lynch took the ride across Toberona Bridge to the Devil's Drop hill. He had spent most of the afternoon gathering information, trying to find out if the Garda had established any link between Inspector Manley and the murder victims. He couldn't believe that Staunton and his men had just handed the girl over to some unknown party, or that they had taken responsibility for killing Dolan and Byrne. She had already seen him at the UDA safe house, and she would undoubtedly put him on the spot if she were rescued. His only hope at this point was to find out who she was given to and whether they got the job done yet. Until then, he had to keep covering his tracks.

He saw Jack O'Callahan's Bentley parked up on top of the hill, and he was standing by the hood as he watched Joe approach. Lynch cruised up and parked about five yards away from his car, smiling as he got out to meet him. Jack seemed noncommittal and said little over the phone, only that he had new information and wanted to touch bases.

"I came across some interesting info this afternoon," Jack advised him as Joe strolled over. "I just wanted to see if you had anything before I started telling my story."

"Well, not much beside checking out a biker club over on Toberona," Joe shrugged. "I tried to find out if they heard or saw anything down there in the Drop, and I drew a blank. My suspicion is that they'd be the only ones with the sand to go poking around that area after dark. They told me they'd let me know if anything came up, and I kinda doubt they will.""Now, why's that, Joe?" Jack frowned. "I just cut Guillotine Gordon loose along the Crescent just a little while ago. He told me you're their go-to man over at the club. He also said you knew all about him doing the job on Dolan and Byrne."

"You pick up lots of information when you're working the streets, Jack," Joe stuck his hands in his suit pockets, staring out at the sea. "You should know that."

"Lots of things that I should know, but I've just about got all I need," Jack played his bluff. "I've got witnesses that'll testify that you were one of the last ones to have seen Siobhan."

"Why would you need witnesses?" he asked mildly. "You already told me she called you and told you she'd spoken to Leo Blake and Joe Lynch."

"I'm talking about that night, the night she disappeared. I'm taking you in, Joe."

"It won't be that easy, Jack," Joe smirked before he went for his gun. Things had just happened too quick for him to get ready for this. He didn't know how Gordon could have known he was at the safe house while Siobhan was there, but the bikers had too many connections north of the border for him to take a chance. Somebody might have given up the info in exchange for a favor, but regardless of the situation, Joe could not take the risk of Jack putting him on the spot.

Joe kept his Smith and Wesson revolver in a breakaway shoulder holster that he had quick-drawn from on numerous occasions. Yet he was not quite as quick as Jack, who had practiced his draw from the hip as he dropped to a crouch almost weekly as a religious practice on the firing range. Jack caught Joe left of center, putting two slugs in his heart as he staggered backwards and dropped to the ground, rolling down an incline and off the cliff.

Jack walked over to the edge of the cliff and looked down at the broken figure of his adversary. It would take many months of investigations and explanations before the authorities on both sides of the border could reconcile the fact that an Inspector from the Garda Siochana shot another Inspector from the Royal Ulster Constabulary in the heart so that his body would fall into the Devil's Drop.

* * *

Siobhan Manley woke up from her stupor sometime that evening, finding that she had been bound and gagged with duct tape. She focused blurrily and saw a figure sitting on a chair at the side of the cot next to her, staring intently through eyelets in a burlap hood. She struggled feebly before the figure stood up and grabbed her by the arm, pulling her onto the floor. She tried to scream and yell but her jaw was bound tight, and she figured that the tape must have been wrapped tight around the back of her head.

The abductor yanked her up off the ground by her arm as she let loose a muffled cry, but was pulled to her feet and shoved through the bedroom door into the next room. She managed to get her bearings and was horrified by the sight of the older man who she had first thought to be Joe Lynch. Only his throat had been sliced open from ear to ear, and his mouth had been opened wide which indicated that he might have been garroted before he was butchered. The gore had spilled in a torrent down his chest, and from the neck down the corpse seemed as if dipped in blood. Siobhan tried to scream with horror but all she could hear was a distant wail inside her head. Suddenly she felt the burlap hood being put on her head backwards, blocking her vision as she was shoved forward into the cool of the night.

She heard the sound of the trunk of a car being popped, and as she was shoved forth, her knees hit a surface that made her think she was being shoved into the trunk. She began pushing backwards but at once was hit so hard in the back of the head that she lost consciousness.

She had no way of knowing how long she had been unconscious, aware only of a splitting headache and the fact that she was still tied up. She was able to move her legs but could scarcely breathe, realizing that the abductor probably had locked her in what she figured was a car trunk. She began kicking, and at once the trunk flew open. She stared in shock at the hooded figure that had dragged her from the shack, the one who had probably killed Joe Lynch.

"Well, first you don't see me, then you do," he spoke in a cockney accent before grabbing her by the hair by both hands, hauling her out of the trunk and onto the grass. "Sorry I had to keep you waiting so long, but I wanted to make sure we weren't gonna be bothered while we had our little get-together."

He pulled her up by her arm, twisting her shoulder as she gave another muffled cry through the duct tape. He shoved her forth again, and she realized she was in the tree-canopied forest area Leo Blake had described when they first spoke. He pushed her forward through a stand of vine-choked bushes, and she found herself in front of a two-foot stake hammered into the ground. She started to recoil but at once felt a nauseating impact between her shoulder blades. At once her entire upper body felt as if hit by an electric shock before she went completely numb, sagging to the ground like a marionette whose strings had been cut.

"That's what the Yanks used to call a head on a stick over in Vietnam," the hooded man showed her the hand axe that had hit her in the back. "They'd cut the spinal cord so that all that worked was from the neck up. I think that'll keep you here until I can go up and fetch the lady in that house up on that hill. I think you and her and I will have a wonderful time together. At least I know I will."

With that, he produced a rope and tied it around her neck, then tied the other end around the stake almost as an afterthought. She was nearly hysterical with fear, realizing that this psychopath had probably crippled her for life. All she could do was watch his back as he disappeared through the brush, on his way to pay a visit to the lady on the hill.

Chapter Five

Leo Blake breathed in the aroma of the river breeze that permeated the countryside, savoring the day as he made his way around the bend past the treeline not far from the Toberona Bridge. It was a lovely morning and he had a spring in his step, his tackle box feeling a tad lighter today as he went along his way with gusto.

He decided to make his rounds in town before setting about on his task today, stopping in at the general store to pick up a couple of items and passing the craic with the locals. He walked up and down the street as was his custom, chatting with the early-risers and the shopkeepers opening for business. Everyone wished him a great day, hoping that he would bring some choice catches at the end of the day which would allow them to take home a special treat for dinner for a good price. Everyone agreed that Leo Blake making the rounds was as much as part of the morning along the riverside as the sun rising in the east, gulls sailing about diving for breakfast, and cats meowing at the back door for a saucer of milk.

It was slightly after eight AM by the time he headed off towards the river. He took the scenic route going back towards the treeline where the gullies filled with wildlife and contributed greatly to the backwoods atmosphere in the vicinity. He stopped a couple of times and looked around, seeing no one about, then changed his course slightly in heading into the tree-canopied wooded area.

There was something about being out here that was so very special. Sometimes it was all about being one with nature, with the flora and fauna, and if he was the only man on earth. From here, in this private world, he could look out and see the surrounding community and its daily activity. They were unaware they were being watched, studied and even judged, and ultimately it was as if he had the power of life and death over them all.

It made him feel like God.

He reached the west end of the treeline and looked up at the hill where the wooden cottage sat. He knew the lady was there with her little dog, as her jeep was parked out back as it always was when she was home. He decided to go on up there and offer his services, to see if there were any rooms to be painted, any wood to be chopped, any furniture to be moved or any leaks on the roof to be mended. It was well known that she had no phone, so it should not seem unusual to walk up the hill to inquire if one had no vehicle.

He walked around the hill, taking the side road which led to a dirt path along the west end out of view from the riverfront. People would not look out and see Leo Blake trudging up to the cottage and wondering what business he had up there. It would not seem as he was intruding, or being a busybody, of changing his routine in any way. Unless they were using binoculars to watch her home, it would seem as if no one had ever come by this way at all.

By the time he got to the house, it seemed as if deserted with no sign of life about. He had used his own binoculars from time to time and watched her in the yard, playing with her little poodle, throwing its ball which it chased about merrily. It was like a little motor scooter, racing around non-stop, changing its course only when she threw the ball. It would then anchor the ball between its paws and direct the ball back to its mistress' feet.

He sauntered up the path, noticing that the curtains were drawn and did not allow for a view of the inside of the house. It simply would not do for him to peek inside, for that would have been seen as improper regardless of the circumstance. He walked over to the front step and decided to test the doorknob, and to his surprise he found it unlocked. This was now the hour of decision, and he took into consideration that the little dog was not barking wildly as such animals were wont to do. It seemed plausible that one might have found the door unlocked and walked in when not hearing either the lady or her dog about to see if any malfeasance may had occurred.

He heard the click of the bolt and opened the door softly, gently, seeing the highly polished wooden floor and the white flower print of her matching furniture within. He eased it halfway and at once sighted the little dog. It was hopping up and down excitedly, its bobbed tail spinning like a top. Only it could not bark and instead gave out a strange noise like bubble wrap being popped. There was only the weird sound from its throat and the click of its nails on the floor.

Click-click-click. Pop-pop-pop.

He stepped into the house and suddenly he heard a double thump, one from a corner of the room, and a second one as he felt a devastating impact against his midsection. It felt as if he had been kicked in the stomach by a mule, and he had no control whatsoever as he slowly sank to his knees. Through a blurry haze he saw a crossbow in a fixed position attached to a long cord on a rack facing the doorway.

"I was expecting you," the lady emerged from a back room where apparently she had been hiding. She was very calm and collected, and walked into her kitchen as she casually began sorting things on the countertop. "It's just like fishing, I suppose. If you use the right bait and you're patient, something good will come your way. I'm sure you know all about that."

He gazed down at his hands, wrapped around a two-foot section of an arrow sticking out of his belly. He felt the sticky wetness oozing from his shirt, down the front of his trousers, as if he was losing control of his bowels over her carpet. He tried to speak but the impact had taken all the air out of his lungs. He tried to breathe but it was as if the blood was also trying to escape upwards, into his esophagus.

"My sister was Sinead McNamara, who was one of your last victims," she strode over and picked his tackle box off the floor where it had fallen beside him. She stepped around the spreading pool of blood that was starting to seep from his pants, and took the box back to the countertop where she began inspecting its contents. "I see you've brought most of your own things, and that's good. I have a couple of other things of my own."

He saw her inspect the pre-filled morphine syringes in his tackle box as well as the local anesthetics, the bottle of ether and assorted sundries. All the time the little dog danced around in front of him, trying to bark as it avoided the pool of blood.

Click-click-click.Pop-pop-pop.

He realized that she might have had its vocal chords removed, specifically for this occasion. She had planned this out carefully, just as thoroughly as he ever had. She would be just as uncompromising, just as thorough, without remorse. She had put long, hard thought into this, and would never stray from her course. Even if it meant removing her dog's vocal chords.

"The coroner's report indicated you kept my sister alive for about a week," she said, taking the items from his tackle box and arranging them on the countertop. "I assure you I will do my very best to do the same for you."

His mind raced frantically as he considered whatever options might remain available. If the postman, the milkman or anyone else came by, there had been no forcible signs of entry or any indication that Leo Blake had ever come up here at all. He had deliberately come up so that no one would have ever seen him arrive, and it was very possible that no one would ever see him leave. He was growing dizzy from the loss of blood, and the pain in his stomach was encompassing his conscious now. All that remained was the puddle of blood he sat in, the devilish arrow sticking out of his stomach, and the little dog dancing joyfully in front of him.

Click-click-click.Pop-pop-pop.

* * *

At Jack O'Callahan's insistence, the bloodhounds were brought out once again, and this time they found Siobhan Hanley in critical condition tied to a stake in the woods alongside the Toberona Bridge. She was rushed to Louth County Hospital and diagnosed with a serious spinal injury and dehydration, and was in a state of shock. It was determined that the axe blow to her spine was a C6 injury, which had caused paralysis of her body and legs that might possibly be corrected by surgery. There was also a possibility of autonomic dysreflexia, which would cause abrupt increases in blood pressure which would require immediate attention. She would be confined to a wheelchair while recuperating, and Jack O'Callahan would be putting in for a leave of absence to devote sufficient time to her recuperative process.

"Hey, pretty girl," he reached out and gently stroked her hair from her face as she gazed up at him through the dark shadows around her eyes. She was pale and her lips were chapped from having gone without water, coupled by the effects of the strychnine.

"You're a sight for sore eyes," she managed. "What's going on in the world?"

"Well, not a whole lot," he admitted. "You didn't give us much to work with."

"After being raped, kidnapped and left in a field by some maniac, plus getting hit in the back with an axe, I don't know how much information the average person tends to retain," she was sarcastic.

"We found the rapists up on that hill, and the forensics report corroborated your story," Jack said, his heart moved by the forlorn sight of her. "We don't know where that UDA safe house you were taken to was located, but we suspect it was somewhere in South Armagh. I got some evidence against Joe Lynch and confronted him with it, and he pulled a gun on me. I shot him in self-defense and they're tying me to a desk until the investigation's over. I'm using you as an excuse to get out of the office until the smoke clears."

"You're much too kind, Jack."

"You know I love you," he held her hand softly in his. "I always have, always will."

"I know," she squeezed his hand, her eyes misty. "See, you're making me cry, now stop."

"You'll be up and around in no time," he assured her. "They've got some of the finest neurosurgeons in the UK looking at this. They say that the fact that you survived the first twenty-four hours after the injury without treatment indicates there's an excellent chance of survival."

"What does *that* mean?"

"Most people don't survive those kind of injuries, love," he said quietly.

"Has anyone checked on that lady who lives on the hill?" she wondered.

"Aye, we sent a patrol car up there right after we found you. She says everything's been quiet as usual and that she hadn't seen anything unusual. The postman indicates she's always very pleasant when he drives by, and he never sees anything out of the ordinary. She also comes down to the general store every now and again, and that's always like a special event with all the fellows falling over each other trying to help her. Did you hear any of those bastards who attacked you mention her?"

"No, not at all," she said quietly. "I was drugged, and they poisoned me at one point. I don't remember much of anything."

"That fellow Leo Blake's gone missing as well," Jack revealed. "They went up to his cottage and found it deserted. After nobody'd seen him for three days they called the Garda to look into it. They've got a missing persons alert out for him now. You've been in the headlines for the past week. All of Ireland's been praying for you."

"Was there anything about someone impersonating Joe Lynch?" she wondered.

"No, but I can look into it," he assured her as the nurse approached from the corridor. "You go ahead and get some rest, darling. I'm thinking they want to give you another oil change."

"Love you, Jack."

"Love you too."

It was over a week before the residents along the Dundalk riverfront were of the general consensus that Leo Blake had become a victim of foul play. He was sorely missed by all, not only for his friendly personality and helpful attitude, but the delightful catches he brought in after a good day of fishing. Many prayers were offered up, along with novenas and eventually masses for the salvation of his soul. Most were saddened by the loss of their neighbor, and at night in some homes there could be heard weeping and the gnashing of teeth.

About two weeks after the disappearance of Leo Blake, the residents noticed the arrival of a moving van at the top of the hill not far from Toberona Bridge. It took them most of the afternoon to load her belongings onto the truck, and by sunset the little jeep followed the truck onto Toberona Bridge on into Dundalk.

Without further ado, the lady on the hill was never seen or heard of again.

Chapter Six

Kids in the Park

It was Christmas Eve, and Jon Farrow was walking on air on his way home from the office. There was a light snow flurry coming down, and it set the mood for what he expected to be a most memorable holiday season. He was presenting Christine Thornton with a $10,000 engagement ring, and it was definitely something that was going to impress her. Lots of her girlfriends had gotten married over the past few months with the biological clock ticking. They had shown her some impressive jewelry in the process, but Jon was not to be outdone.

He had an awesome year in the middle of the Great Recession, selling more stock than anyone at Powers and Wood, one of the fastest-growing brokerages in NYC. He had focused on alternative energy, selling more stock in windmill manufacturers and recycling industries than anyone in the company. He could really pitch the stuff ("It's the wave of the *future*! Think of what you're contributing to our country's *future*!"), and had people not only investing in what they thought was a get-rich-quick deal, but believing in what they were doing. It was a helluva lot better than selling foreclosures, though deep down Jon Farrow didn't really give a damn either way.

Christine was a real estate broker who had made some huge scores on the real estate market over the year. Her own angle was getting investors to bid against one another, finding two speculators to go head-to-head over foreclosed properties until she was the only person left standing once it was over. She was the top scorer at Conley and Glass, and had even been named by *Forbes Magazine* as one of the Top 100 fastest-rising female brokers in NYC. Theirs would be a marriage made in heaven, with both partners at the top of their game and still moving on up.

Yet the theme song of their relationship might very well have been, "What's Love Got to Do With It". The sex was fantastic and they cared for each other tremendously, but deep down he suspected that money was their first love. They had left each other's beds so often at the break of dawn at the call of a cell phone that they could have easily been mistaken for doctors or lawyers. It had been the reason they never discussed long-term plans, but he felt as if a change was coming. He had a longing for something more stable, and he suspected that she might have felt the same way too.

He had the cabbie circle the block, having found the curb alongside his condo apartment building surrounded by double-parked cars. Snow flurries were beginning to blanket the area with a light coating, and he really didn't want to walk through ice water along the curb with his new shoes. Yet it seemed like he did not have much choice in the matter, and gave the cabbie a $20 for a ten-dollar fare before negotiating the puddle at the corner to make the sidewalk.

Never the sentimental type, he had totally bought into the Japanese concept of a disposable society. It seemed to him that mankind had gone full cycle, and the truth its ancestors knew back at the dawn of civilization was now a concept the world was getting reacquainted with. Prehistoric man had not filled his cave with useless junk. That which outlived its usefulness was thrown away. Sentimentality was a curse of the industrial age, people keeping mementos of a past that they could never relive.

Christmastime seemed to give one pause to reflect on such things, being the most sentimental time of the year. People spent all their time and energy trying to find the perfect gift, something that the recipient would treasure most at the least expense. Most of the time it was an item the intended could well do without. Yet they would cherish it anyway since it was the hypocritical thought that counted. They would wear the grotesque article of clothing, display the horrid piece of bric-a-brac, or show off the half-hearted handicraft every single Christmas to rub it in the giver's face forever and ever. Even more farcical was the anger and shame of the giver when they received something they believed was of even lesser value.

He had made a pretty good score over the years by changing out his own art collection every year. He would go down to Soho and buy it at some starving artist's exhibit one year, then open his own sale and let it go at a decent profit, then repeat the process. He made it a rule to never invest more than his original stake, and as it was his collection had grown in value tenfold without him ever having lost a dime. That was the way of the world. Yesterday's Cabbage Patch Doll bought for $100 years ago was sitting in a Salvation Army bin today. One man's treasure was another man's trash. Art was something you moved around before the somebody you bought the artwork from became a nobody.

That was what he and Christine had so much in common. They went through life like a bottle of wine, sipping, swirling, savoring and swallowing, then going on to find an even better one. He knew they spent a lot of time looking over each other's shoulders when they were locked in each other's embrace, but he was pretty sure those days were over. You couldn't go around the lot kicking tires forever, and most of the time the car you drove off with was the one you laid eyes on in the first place. She was the one, and he knew that if she accepted this deal she would never look back. One thing about Christine was that a deal was a deal was a deal.

Even though he was all about replacing used things with something of equal value or better as soon as they depreciated, he really didn't want to replace these damned shoes so quickly. He dropped $200 for them and regretted the fact that he was not a galoshes type, risking high-ticket Italian leather in ice water rather than be seen pulling off rubber boots from his feet like some janitor protecting the only shoes he owned. He wasn't into wastage, and disdained those who threw money away without realizing the happiness it bought in life.

He considered the little beggar who sat along the curbside just ahead. He felt nothing but disgust for those who stood on street corners with WORK FOR FOOD signs, yet thought they were way smarter than the whores on the streets selling their asses for the same kind of money. Still, anyone who went through life looking for handouts was living exactly the kind of life they deserved. He always knew that the harder you worked in the beginning, the less you worked in the end. Anyone on Social Security could tell you how that worked. Yet it was those like this kid who never had a chance to work who deserved the pity. Nothing from nothing leaves nothing, and this kid deserved more from his parents than a chance to sit in the gutter in the snow trying to make a buck to get through the night.

"Mister, can you spare a quarter? Mister, spare a quarter?"

The kid looked like he came from India, with jet black hair and ebon skin, wearing a threadbare hoodie over a faded T-shirt and torn denims, along with the cheap black PF Flyers he didn't even think they sold anymore. He visibly shook with cold, and he had a plastic cup that had some chump change and a couple of singles in it. He didn't look like he weighed ninety-eight pounds soaking wet, which he would probably be if the snow got any wetter.

Jon saw street charity as one of the biggest scams on earth. He knew how many hands went into those Salvation Army kettles before the poor got the leftovers at the bottom. He knew how the street corner guys lived off their daily take, cashing their welfare checks at the end of the month for their First Friday sex, liquor and drug jamborees. Even the Sisters of Charity brought their take back to the Church, who kicked their proceeds back to the Diocese, which kicked the lion's share back to the Vatican. As they said, you give a man a fish and you feed him for a day, so he's up and around to go begging again tomorrow.

"Mister, got a quarter?"

He stopped and absent-mindedly pulled a fiver out of his wallet, looking down at the kid, who seemed to have some kind of caul over his left eye. He also appeared to have a harelip and cold sores, all of which reflected bad genetics and a deprived background. There wasn't anything in Jon's past that had gotten him a free ride from Flatbush to Wall Street, just like there wasn't anything that was going to get this kid off the curb to decent room and board tonight.

"Gee, thanks, mister," the kid smiled up at him. He had Bridgman eyes and teeth, and he was healthy enough to survive if he just had a chance. Maybe some rich old geezer would share some holiday cheer and give the kid that lucky break. Hell, they said Indian kids were good at math. Maybe in a boys' home with computer access, this kid might be opening his own research lab in Silicon Valley one day.

"Happy holidays, kid," Jon managed a smile and headed off to the canopied entrance at 768 Fifth Avenue at the Plaza Residences. It was one of the most exclusive condo high-rises in Manhattan, overlooking Central Park with a great view of the Plaza and the Pulitzer Fountain. Christine was overjoyed by Jon's two million-dollar investment, and though he got into some serious debt, he finally got a grip on it and was truly reaping what he had sown. He never lost the thrill of leaving the office at the end of the day and returning to what was truly home sweet home. He always thought of this place as his reward for risking financial disaster in gambling everything for it. He thought of it as proof positive that anyone could accomplish anything if they put everything they had into it. He could not pity someone who couldn't put a roof over their own head if he had used catastrophe as the engine that constructed his. Yet he could not help but feel sorry for that kid.

He approached the carpeted threshold where the doorman waited at the glass revolving door, not even having a door to hold open. Jon was in an oddly reflective mood tonight and paused to consider that he had never given doormen their due. Perhaps he thought it unseemly that a man would take a job kissing ass all the days of his life. Those who cleaned and tended the rooms had usually come to terms with their stations in life and gave thanks that they had a wonderful place to clean up. Standing around and kissing ass as the door was just not what Jon considered noble.

"Evening, Jeeves," Jon smiled, then paused to look back at the boy.

"Good evening, Mr. Farrow," he was given a toothy grin.

At once he saw a man emerge from the shadows and, after a brief exchange, reach down to take the beggar's cup. The boy resisted him, and was given a punch to the head before it was taken from him. The thief ran away with the cup as the boy laid in the slush and did not move.

"Hey!" Jon yelled. "Hey!" He then turned to the doorman. "Did you see that?"

"They steal from each other all the time, sir. It is truly sad."

"He just hit that kid!" Jon stared indignantly at the doorman before rushing out to where the boy laid.

"Be careful, Mr. Farrow!" the doorman warned him. "Sometimes they run a scam where the other one's still waiting!"

Jon was taken aback by the skepticism of such a notion as he ran down the marbled steps and rushed to where the boy lay about thirty yards away. The boy seemed dazed and lay weeping on the sidewalk, doubtlessly over the hopelessness of his lot. Jon squatted down and put him hand on the boy's shoulder.

"Hey, fella, c'mon, sit up. Are you okay?"

"He took all my money," the boy wept.

"C'mon, get up," Jon softly tugged at his arm until he sat upright. "Can you walk? Maybe you should get off the street for a couple of minutes."

He rationalized it as similar to having watched a car knock down a cat or a dog in the middle of the street. Even here, on Fifth Avenue, where some of the most cold-blooded sons-of-bitches on the planet dwelled, no one would dare show their true colors by discouraging someone from rescuing the animal from the middle of the road. Regardless of this being a raggedy urchin, no one would dare say that he was not even worth the kindness one would show an animal.

"Sir, I don't know that you want to bring him inside," the doorman came over as Jon held the boy around the shoulders. He could not have been more than thirteen, and he was short and scrawny due to lack of nutrition. "Leave him here with me and I'll get him a blanket and coffee while I send for the police."

"It's freezing out here," Jon snapped at him. "He's not an animal, he's a human being. He can sit inside until he gets himself together."

"Mr. Farrow, even if I ignore him, there will be at least a dozen other employees who will call security as soon as they lay eyes on him," the doorman said earnestly.

"Fine, then," Jon said tautly. "I'll take him upstairs and let him pull himself together."

"Please be careful, Mr. Farrow."

"No problem, Jeeves."

"Jenkins, sir."

"Pardon?"

"Jenkins, sir. My name is Jenkins."

"Right."

Jon ushered the boy towards the golden elevators at the end of the cavernous lobby with its enormous chandeliers hanging impossibly from the ceilings as if in the gardens of Babylon. Guests passing them by glanced disapprovingly at the boy before looking up at Jon with a benign smile and a nod of approval. It gave him a twisted sense of satisfaction, knowing that their hypocrisy was allowing him to rub this little beggar right in their faces.

"I'll get you a cup of coffee," Jon smiled down at the ugly little face, filled with gratitude for his generosity. "I probably have some cookies around somewhere. You know how it is this time of year, people giving you boxes and packages of stuff it takes months to eat. I'll give you some to take with you."

"You are so generous, I thank you with all my heart, *sahib*," the boy said earnestly.

"Wow, *sahib*. I haven't heard that one since I was a kid," Jon chuckled as he patted the boy's shoulder, the elevator door opening at the twelfth floor. "Must've been in a movie."

He walked the boy to the end of the hall where his suite was, affording him a magnificent view of the Manhattan skyline. He opened the door and stepped inside, proudly flicking on the light and letting the boy take in the view of his palatial abode.

"Not bad, eh?" Jon asked with a big grin.

"Very beautiful, *sahib.*"

"By the way, my name's Jon. What's yours?"

"Damodar," he replied. "It is a name of the Lord Krishna."

"Of course," John muttered. "Go on and have a seat on the couch, the one by the window, make yourself comfortable. You can open up some of those packages on the table, see if you can find some cookies. Now, don't forget, I keep my gifts, you get the munchies."

"Yes, Jon. Thank you very much."

The boy seemed to be strangely at home amidst the Louis XV furnishings. Jon thought it odd because he remembered feeling as if he was in a museum the first time he came into one of these suites. Damodar chose the ornate table by the window, pulling the white curtain back so he could enjoy the view of Central Park south while he inspected the packages on the marbled table in the center of the room bracketed by two embroidered, brass-framed chairs. The boy was so poorly dressed that it would have been impossible for him to steal something without it bulging from his threadbare clothing.

Jon headed for the steel refrigerator and began searching around, rummaging through the fruit and vegetables Christine insisted he keep on hand. She probably couldn't cook worth a damn but sure could whip up some great salads. Like she said, it kept them healthy, slim and trim, but that wasn't going to cut it for this poor kid. He hated the idea of having to give him just a cup of coffee, but you couldn't give what you didn't have.

Jon could hear him rustling around in the living room, then it grew quiet as he probably found something good to eat. Jon figured he would let the kid sleep it off until Christine got there, then they could make arrangements to have him taken to a good shelter somewhere.

He never expected the small hand to grab him by the hair from behind as he squatted before the refrigerator, the needle plunging into his neck and knocking him out cold.

Chapter Seven

Jon came around a short time later, still groggy but able to focus on the thin figure standing before him. He had been dragged to the overstuffed sofa in the living room, and he found his wrists and ankles had been bound with plastic quick-ties.

"There you are, coming around at last," Damodar stood with hands on hips, admiring his handiwork. "I want to make this as painless as possible, so don't make any efforts to yell or create a commotion or I will have to gag you and secure you further."

"Okay, look," Jon relented, "you got me. Go ahead and call your gang and take whatever you want. My girlfriend's on her way over here. When she gets here the situation is gonna get way out of hand. Go ahead and take what you can, but you'd better get going right now."

"Why, it's Christmas Eve," he replied, walking over to the sofa and sitting down comfortably, his little feet barely touching the ground. "People are in for the evening. In a few hours I'll be able to walk out of here and no one will hardly notice."

"A few hours!" Jon snapped. "I told you my girlfriend's on her way over here! You better get the hell out now before you get in some deep shit, buddy!"

"You mean you don't consider this deep shit?" Damodar smiled back. "Here you are, tied up in your fabulous penthouse suite in midtown Manhattan, having been drugged with a fast-acting sedative which is still in your bloodstream. If the authorities were to come across us at this very moment, that would be enough to deport me back to India."

"So why the hell are you taking this risk, kid?" Jon reasoned. "Okay, look, let's just blow this off. You saw an opportunity and you took it, but now you've painted yourself into a corner. Go ahead and grab whatever you want. I got a few bucks in my wallet. I wouldn't take the plastic because it'll be useless in a couple of hours, but I'm sure you already know that. You can check those presents, if you see something of value—which I'm sure you already have—go on and grab it. By the time my girlfriend gets here you'll already be on the subway."

"This is what is admirable about you, and that's why someone would want to be you," Damodar allowed. "You are very goal-oriented, very objective, with wisdom and perception beyond your years. You have been proven yourself worthy of going on to do great things in a different stage of reincarnation."

"Okay, hold on," Jon insisted. "I know you Hindus believe that when people die, they go on to a different life."

"That is true, that is the essence of the universe. Nothing ever dies, it merely disintegrates, and its particles are rearranged to become part of something greater, something new. Our spirits are the force that brings these things to life. We never truly die, we simply move on and become what other human beings recognize as someone else."

"So what the hell are you talking about, you're thinking of killing me?" Jon scoffed.

"Let's just say that you and I will be advancing to different stages of our spiritual journeys," Damodar replied. "I can no longer remain where I am, and unfortunately, this situation will have repercussions for you, It is all a matter of predestination."

"Look, kid, let's talk this over. I don't know what kind of shit some Brahma or guru or whatever crammed inside your head, but if you kill me, I'm not going anywhere but six feet under. And as for you, they'll throw you in prison for murder. When the press gets hold of how you got in here—and the doorman will testify to it—they'll throw you in jail for the rest of your life. And let me tell you something, pal, a little shit like you will get put on booty duty so quick, your asshole will be the size of a silver dollar before the week's out."

"I seriously doubt that will be the case, but I'm happy if that brings you some consolation."

"Okay, let's back this up," Jon tried again. "I'm here, you're there, you've got the upper hand. I've got no problem with you walking out of here like this never happened. If you make this any worse, especially when my girlfriend gets here, you'll have created a problem for yourself that you won't be able to fix. Right now you're in control, you can still make the best choice."

"And what makes you think I won't be in control when she gets here?"

"Wait a second," Jon's eyes widened. "You're waiting for her to get here? You can't be that stupid. She's gonna be an innocent victim, she's got no part in this."

"Well, what do you consider yourself?"

"Look, give it to me straight. What in hell do you want? Obviously I've got money, I can get you squared away any way you like. If we can get to an ATM, I'll give you the codes and get you all the cash you need. Just leave her out of this."

"I told you already, and I know you're having trouble getting a grip on it. I'm in what you might call a desperate need for your soul, and there's no getting around it. I looked you up on the Internet, and it was a careful selection on my part. Both you and your girlfriend had the ideal souls that I would need to go on to the next evolution."

"What the hell are you trying to say? You're planning to kill Christine too?"

"As I explained to you, no one ever dies in this universe we live in. We simply go on to other stages of existence. Your Western science validates that. If someone were to plunge a dagger into your heart, you would actually feel yourself leave your body. It would hover by a ectoplasmic thread, similar to your umbilical cord. Once the thread was finally broken, you would be free to go on to your next incarnation. It is happening billions of times over as we speak, from the microbe world to our very own."

"Listen, kid, you can't go around thinking your religious convictions are gonna do a damned thing for you in the real world," Jon was adamant. "It's a great thing for little old men and ladies who are getting ready to meet their maker. For people like us with a lot of time left on the clock, thinking that far ahead can lead to terrible mistakes. Look at those Muslims over there in the Middle East. They've been told that dying for Allah gets them straight to heaven where a thousand virgins are standing around naked waiting for them. Only they get arrested or captured and end up in prison for the rest of their lives, in hell holes like Abu Ghraib and Guantanamo Bay. If I believed all that stuff, I'd be begging for you to kill me so I could go to heaven and sit around on a cloud playing the harp forever and ever. Reality sucks, kid, and the reality is that if you kill me, I go to the morgue and you go to prison for life."

"It's sad that you have come to this point in life and never truly come to terms with what it is really all about," Damodar was wistful. "Perhaps you had in a previous existence, but your stubbornness is blinding and deafening you to the spiritual things, the truly important things in life. Your only desire is for the things of the material world, the things that you cannot take with you. If only you had focused on the living things, the plants, the trees, the animals, other people, you might not have chosen this path that allowed me to stumble over you."

"There, you said you stumbled over me. Why don't you leave here and stumble over somebody else? I've never been enlightened before, I've never had the benefit of a swami or a guru like you have. Can't you see, the Lord Krishna has sent you to me in order to enlighten me. If you let me mend my ways, I can help Christine get her act together as well. I'd even agree to go join a Hindu temple somewhere. I can give your people a lot of money and help a lot of people find the true spiritual path."

"Spoken like a true salesman, Jon," Damodar chuckled. "It is easy to see how you have come so far in this life. Always trying to adapt and overcome, rapidly assimilating facts and synthesizing them into an ideal solution. In Christine you have found a kindred spirit. She finds some poor soul who has mortgaged his future for a dream home for his family—much like you did when you first moved in here. Only he does not have the same karma as you and loses everything. Yet, before his credit crashes and burns once and forever, she beats the deadline and sinks him into twice the debt with another ninety days to cheat the hangman."

"Hold on. How do you know what Christine does for a living?"

"I told you, I have researched you both carefully and found that you would both be perfect for my next evolution."

"What are you going to need the both of us for?"

"Two voyages, two vessels," Damodar replied.

"What do you mean, two voyages?" Jon demanded. "You mean you have somebody else in on this deal?"

"Yes, I am afraid so. Sometimes it is very difficult continuing on in one's journey leaving behind the one you love. Now, it is entirely possible that if your connection with Christine is as strong as you believe it is, you may be reunited in the next life, and surely you will know. There are those who become clairvoyant, and can remember certain details from a past life. If the Lord Krishna desires, you may well meet each other again and continue your journey anew."

"Listen, you sick little shit," Jon struggled against his bonds, "you lay a hand on Christine and I swear I'll kill you. This shit's gone on long enough. At least a dozen people saw you come up here, and there is no way in hell an ugly little shit like you can go anywhere on earth without being recognized. They will track you down and lock you up forever, and you're gonna be old and gray, living in hell waiting for a nirvana which will never come!"

"Let me ask you this," Damodar postulated. "Judging by our conversation, would you comfortably assume that I accumulated all this knowledge as a beggar on the streets of New York City? Or even if I had come straight from India, do you think one so deformed would have been accepted among the Brahmins (*upper caste)? Have you factored this into your hypothesis?"

"No, I was hoping you might enlighten me on how you came to be so smart and so stupid at the same time," Jon was sarcastic.

"Actually, this all began in the court of King Louis XIV," Damodar explained. "That is why I found it so ironic that your furnishings reflect the environment of his successor. There was a certain Madame de Montespan who made her way into his court and his bedchambers by way of mystical spells and potions she used to put the king under her influence. There was quite a bit of witchery going on in those days, and the Madame brought a large number of courtesans into the inner circle who she had tutored in the forbidden arts. One of them was Charlotte Dupree, who just happened to be a close acquaintance of mine. We were lovers, I should say."

"Holy shit," Jon was astonished. "So that's what this is all about. Some scumsucking maharajah in Hinduland got you so doped up he made you think you're the reincarnation of some French nobleman. Okay, kid, listen to this. I can get you through this. It's some kind of brainwash mind control technique, plain and simple. He's programmed you to locate middle class Americans and do them in for their money. I can guarantee you that you're not the only one. Get me loose and I swear to you, we'll search to the ends of the earth to catch the bastards and put *them* away for life."

"Jon, I'm not opening a corner of the bag to let you out, I'm merely trying to help you come to terms with what is happening here," Damodar shook his head. "You can either work yourself into a state of panic and go to the next life as a self-pitying hysteric, or you can accept your fate and actually lead Christine into a blissful state of transition. The choice is yours."

"All right, let's play the game," Jon's mind was racing. He knew Christine was on the way as the clock on the wall showed it was about 9:30. She said she had some last-minute shopping to do and would be by as soon as she dropped her purchases off at her place. Since she had a villa out on Long Island, she would be catching a late ferry back to South Street and catch a cab to get over here. The traffic was nauseating at this time of year but a seasoned West Indian cabbie could make it in a half hour. "I'm assuming your partner is Charlotte Dupree. Who are you supposed to be, the Marquis de Sade?"

"You are a funny man, Jon," Damodar gave him a small smile. "I am Jean-Guy Perrault, a man of middle-class beginnings who also took up the study of the black arts as a way to resolve the economic instability and political turmoil of the times. Charlotte and I met in the court of King Louis, and we were considered quite skilled in the arts by none other than the Madame herself. We had an Indian *pandit* among us, and Charlotte and I began studying exclusively under his guidance. You see, there are many paths leading to the powers of darkness, and the Great Kali is just one of the many gods of the netherworld."

"Okay, so you and Charlotte bought into this deal," Jon continued to barter for time. If he heard Christine's key in the door, he could create enough of a ruckus for her to realize something was amiss and make a run for it. Christine was born and raised in Queens, and she knew the streets well enough to snap when something seemed to be going sideways. "So let's suppose the Great Kali empowered you to some extent. How did you end up here in this time and place?"

"Unfortunately when you choose a path such as this, you become a slave to the demonic power, much as your Christian Bible refers to its adherents as being servants of Christ," Damodar reflected. "It is even comparable to falling in love with a cold and cynical woman. The demands grow greater and there is less reciprocity as time goes on. Yet eventually you have invested so much time and resources in the relationship that you cannot bring yourself to cut your losses. In our case, we released the lives of a man and woman to the glory of Kali before we were driven from the court of King Louis, and lived as nobles through the reign of his grandson, Louis XV. We were forced to sacrifice once again to escape the French Revolution, and by taking the bodies of German nobles, we were able to migrate to Prussia and access the court of Frederick the

Great. Alas, this can and will turn into a long, drawn-out history lesson. I'm sure you can think of other things to ruminate upon before your appointed time."

"Let's try this on for size," Jon offered. "You know how there are thousands of people around the world who get those *deja vu* episodes where they remember things in places they've never been to before. Maybe this is going on with you, and it's not anything that's never happened to anyone else before. I have no doubt that you have these memories of Jean-Guy Perrault in your head. I'm with you all the way. What I'm asking—begging you—is not to let this get out of hand. You're only a kid, you got your whole life ahead of you. Just let Christine go. When she gets here, I'll tell her I've got a situation and I'll call her. It's happened before with us, trust me. And I'll sit here with you as long as it takes, Damodar. I know you're worth a lot more than what you've gotten in life so far. I brought you up here, and I won't turn my back on you now."

"You are such a good person, I can detect the sincerity in your words, though motivated by your survival instinct, which is as it should be," Damodar folded his hands. "I—"

At once the front door clicked and swung open, and Christine Thornton appeared in the doorway with a tiny Indian girl at her side. Christine was a lovely girl with long black hair, pale blue eyes and alabaster legs that appeared as if chiseled from stone.

"What on earth?" she exclaimed, her eyes wide at the sight of Jon lying prone on the carpet.

"Lakshmi!" Damodar exclaimed.

At that, Christine felt a stabbing sensation in the back of her knee, and at once her legs buckled as she dropped dizzily to the floor.

Chapter Eight

Christine began coming around about a half hour later, and like Jon, she was still groggy but able to focus. She found her wrists and ankles also tied by plastic quick-locks, and someone had the courtesy to pull her dress down so that it covered her knees. She found herself lying on the carpet alongside Jon, and the two Indian kids seated on the couch alongside one another.

"You really look terrible, Jean-Guy," the girl giggled. She was also dressed in rags, with long stringy black hair framing an oval skull with large chestnut eyes and an ugly slit for a mouth.

"You have looked much better in other times yourself," he smiled back as he held her hands affectionately. "I believe that, after midnight, we will be enjoying each other far better."

"Don't start coveting your neighbor's wife until she actually belongs to you," the little girl, whose name was Lakshmi, rebuked him. "I don't want you lusting after her while I am trapped in this body."

"What the hell are they talking about?" Christine demanded, struggling against her ties.

"They're part of some whacked-out Hindu cult," Jon muttered. "He thinks they're gonna be able to inhabit our bodies."

"Jon, this is assault and battery, and they'll probably throw an abduction charge in on top of it," she insisted, her eyes blazing. "I don't care who they're tied in with, they're not getting away with this."

"My dear, I have already covered this ground with Jon before you got here," Damodar said kindly. "This will all be over before you know it. At midnight of the land which we inhabit at the appointed time, we are required to release two souls to their next evolution just as we go on to ours. It will be entirely painless, this I guarantee."

Within twelve days of the Fast of Tevet, at the midnight hour of the land which the believers inhabit, the sacrifice must be made so that the old bodies are cast aside and the new life may begin.

—The Rituals of Diabolus

"Is this little insect trying to say he's going to kill us?" Christine turned to Jon in alarm.

"That's what he's been trying to tell me for the last two hours," Jon frowned. "I'm trying to convince him that they'll put him in jail for the rest of his life for this. Obviously he doesn't care about himself, but hopefully he'll change his mind on behalf of his little friend."

"Have you been tormenting this poor fool for all this time, giving him false hope that he can bargain his way out of this?" Lakshmi rebuked Damodar. "Why did you not gag him and place him in the back room so that he can make peace with himself?"

"They are unbelievers, my darling," he replied. "How cruel is it to take a man's home from him, then cast him into the darkness without so much as a lantern to find his new path?"

"And you believe that you are going to enlighten this simpleton in a matter of hours, to give him an inkling of what has taken us several lifetimes to acquire?" she demanded.

"How did you go about getting involved with her?" Jon asked as Lakshmi and Damodar debated amongst themselves.

"I was at the ferry terminal and I saw her begging on a park bench by the entrance," Christine said ruefully. "I was stupid enough to feel sorry for her, and I went over and put some money in her bowl. The next thing I knew, some gangbanger ran by and hit her and stole her money. I went back over and tried to help, and she asked me if I could pay her way across in case the mugger came back. I rode across with her, and when I found out she had no place to stay, I got the crazy idea of bringing her here so we could find somewhere to send her. The one time in my life I feel sorry for some gutter trash, on Christmas Eve yet, and look what it gets me."

"It was almost the exact same thing that happened to me," he told her. "Look, we've got to put our heads together and find the right button to push. He's part of some reincarnation cult. He thinks that he's going to kill us and inhabit our bodies. Bringing the little girl into the picture gives us additional leverage. He's got it all figured out as far as his own involvement goes, but if we make him realize what he's exposing the girl to, maybe he'll change his mind."

"What do you mean, the same thing happened to you?"

Jon next explained how he gave money to Damodar on the street before he was attacked, just as Christine had done with Lakshmi, and made the same mistake of offering him refuge.

"Okay, now," she said cautiously, "how the hell did they both pull the same scam on both of us in two different boroughs at two different times? How did they know when we would be coming along at the times we did, and how could have they known we knew each other? And if they knew so much about us, what would have made them think that we would have simultaneously made such stupid blunders by taking in a couple of street beggars?"

"I can answer that," Lakshmi smiled, the two kids having halted their own conversation to listen in on Jon and Christine. "It was the Great Kali who told us exactly who you were, how we might find you, and what would happen when we crossed your path. We were able to do some research on Mr. Jon Farrow and Ms. Christine Thornton on the Internet, of course, and that merely satisfied us as to the wisdom of Kali's guidance. Perhaps in your next life you will be given the gift of déjà vu, and it will lead you to the path of enlightenment in undertaking the study of the forces of darkness."

"You think you're gonna kill me? I'll tear your hair out, you little bitch!" Christine flared, jerking violently but unable to break the quick-locks.

"The little bastard got the industrial strength," Jon advised her. "I've been working at it for two hours, they're unbreakable."

"I certainly hope she takes your advice," Lakshmi came over, causing Christine to recoil as she caressed her leg. "Her skin is so smooth, so beautiful. I certainly will enjoy bathing myself far more than I do in this pathetic form."

"Get away from me, you stinking little wretch!" Christine hissed.

"Okay, Lakshmi," Jon tried to buy some more time, "why don't you tell me about the Madame de Montespan? How did she get you tied up in this?"

"Actually the Madame was a mere connection along the way," Lakshmi revealed. "It was Catherine Monvoisin, otherwise known as La Voisin, who got us where we needed to be. She was the leader of our coven and the Madame's spiritual mentor. She was the one who brought us into Louis XIV's court, and that is how we came to meet the Maharaja Shankar. The Maharaja was well-steeped in the knowledge of the Great Kali, and though our fellow witches and warlocks tried to convince us to ignore that path of enlightenment, we studied under Shankar in secrecy. La Voisin tried to dissuade us from continuing our studies as she realized we were growing more powerful than her. Unfortunately, it was discovered that La Voisin and her followers had conspired to poison the Duchasse d'Orleans, who was a rival in the King's court. La Voisin was sentenced to death, but we were able to avail ourselves of the power of the Great Kali and escape."

"And that's when you kidnapped the German couple and fled to Prussia."

"No, we were just fine after we took possession of the French nobles throughout the reign of King Louis XV," she explained, then turned to Damodar. "Did you actually explain all this to him? I actually believe he tried to change the facts around to confuse me. Perhaps there is hope for him in the next life."

"What in hell are they babbling about?" Christine muttered. "Are they on drugs?"

"He's got her locked in as tight as he is," Jon replied quietly. "They've got this story memorized inside out. We're not gonna get them to snap into reality. We've gotta figure out another angle. They're not gonna do whatever it is they're planning until midnight, so we've got a little over an hour to work this out."

"So do you really think that we will be able to resume their daily lives, being as unfamiliar as we are with this world of theirs?" Lakshmi asked as if she were speaking in front of uncomprehending domestic animals. "You know we were nearly murdered in Calcutta before we took the bodies of these urchins. We did not have sufficient time to prepare from the previous incarnation, and it nearly cost us our lives."

"That was because we had to flee from Islamabad after that dispute with the Taliban," he grew testy. "How on earth could I have expected the clumsy Americans to put us in harm's way with their stupid pro-government prattle? We didn't experience those kind of problems in England, or anywhere in Europe. One can't expect what they haven't encountered before."

"Hold on," Christine challenged him. "If you were in Islamabad, then you knew a Roger Bear."

"Roger Bear," Damodar wrinkled his brow in retrospect.

"She must be talking about Captain Bear, that fellow who came through the village where we had that contracting deal," Lakshmi's eyes widened. "That was when all the trouble began. He was the one who told us that if the Taliban continued to strong-arm us for building supplies and payoffs, the Army would protect us. That was before the American dogs abandoned the village and the Taliban bombed our project site."

"Oh my gosh," Christine's blood ran cold as she broke into a cold sweat. "She couldn't have known that. Jon, she couldn't have known that!"

"Known what?" Jon asked as the kids looked on with interest.

"I told you when we first met, that time we were talking about the war, that I had an uncle who got killed over there. It was my Uncle Roger, and he was stationed there with Special Forces on a classified mission. They could've never looked that up on the Internet. They couldn't have known that unless they were there," Christine's voice trembled.

"So you must have been about ten years old at the time," Jon probed.

"It was a different incarnation," Damodar explained patiently. "We had taken the souls of a Pakistani couple while we were trying to escape from Iraq. We were on a Blackwater executive consultant team in Fallujah and inadvertently ordered the massacre of several civilians who we believed were working for Al Qaida. We sacrificed the Pakistanis to Kali and immediately escaped to Islamabad. After we ran into trouble with the Taliban we migrated to Calcutta. There we ran afoul of the Indians when we tried to make contact with fellow worshippers of Kali. They called us heretics because we appeared as Pakis and tried to kill us. We just managed to sacrifice these two waifs you see before you in order to escape. We were desperate after that, and managed to sneak aboard a ship as stowaways to come here to America. It was through the grace of Kali that we were guided to you."

"So what happens next," Jon blurted out, not thinking of Christine. "Are you going to sacrifice us to the devil?"

"What the non-believer worships is despised by the enlightened as foolishness, and what the believer recognizes as the almighty power of darkness is feared by the ignorant as a devil!" Lakshmi derided him. "If your God is the one true God as we have been hearing endlessly over two centuries, then why is He letting you die and giving place to the power of the Great Kali? Why is He forsaking you so that we might be saved?"

"Look, I don't know what kind of brainwashing you've been through or what kind of drugs you've taken to make you buy into this bullshit, but enough is enough!" Christine fumed. "Maybe you found out something about my uncle that makes your story work, but it's not going to let you take over our bodies after you kill us! You're both going to be sitting up here with two dead bodies and no place to hide. Do you think for one minute that all those people who were staring at you when I brought you up here are going to let you just walk out of here with no questions asked? They'll see two beggars walking out of here without the people who brought them in, and they'll know something's wrong. We've got Security Source, when they check on us and see what happened, you'll be spending the rest of your lives in Attica with your sick twisted fantasies."

"Okay, let's think this out," Jon interjected. "You sacrifice us, or whatever you plan to do, and then you have to dispose of those two bodies of yours, after which you next step into our routines to take advantage of this inheritance you've made for yourselves. Lakshmi made a good point earlier. Christine and I are brokers, specialists in our field, not to mention the top sellers for our companies. How do you plan on walking into your offices on Monday and picking up where we left off? According to that fantastic story of yours, it doesn't seem like either of you have had a whole lot of experience selling stock or real estate. Plus how do you get to the money without the bankbooks and passwords?"

"We went through all that as the English couple when we invested our savings in Blackwater," Lakshmi said impatiently. "Banks can't keep your money if you lose all those things. They merely need to establish identity, and being you makes it far easier than pretending to be you."

"You kids are fricking crazy!" Christine screamed. "You can't do this!"

"My dear, if you don't keep your voice down I'll have to gag you," Damodar reprimanded her.

"So what about those bodies you're in right now?" Jon continued. "Does the Great Kali provide for corpse disposal?"

"Once the life source is gone, the bodies simply expire," Damodar explained. "Certainly it will be a curious event, but dressed in these rags in this climate, the authorities would have no choice but to believe that these poor children died of exposure. It would be a rather nice touch for us to start our new lives as good Samaritans having done our best to rescue two unfortunates."

"All right, Damodar, let's cut to the chase," Jon countered. "No matter how well you've been programmed, I know there's a very intelligent kid somewhere in there. You can walk out of here with ten thousand dollars, no questions asked. I've got a diamond ring worth ten grand in my coat pocket. I'll write you out a note and you take it along with the receipt to Zale's first thing in the morning."

The boy walked over to Jon's coat and rifled through its pockets as Christine turned towards Jon in wonderment.

"What diamond ring?" she searched his eyes. "What ten grand?"

"It's an engagement ring I bought for you," he replied softly.

"Oh, Jon," she dissolved into tears.

"This is certainly impressive," Damodar opened the velvet box and inspected the flawless diamond on its platinum band. "I must admit, throughout our travels we have not taken possession of anything like it."

"Let me see," Lakshmi insisted.

"I doubt it'll fit," Damodar frowned. "And you really should wash your hands, darling."

"You get so used to the filth and the grime," Lakshmi burst into tears. "I can't even remember what it is like to be clean anymore, or warm, or pretty."

"You've got feelings, you know what it's like to be a woman," Christine pleaded with Lakshmi. "I've been waiting for something for this all my life, someone to ask me to marry them. I kept giving other things priority in my life until I thought I'd never see the day. Now here I find out that the day has arrived, and you're going to take it away from me? For god's sakes take the ring, take whatever you want, but don't take this away from me. Don't kill me before he can ask me to marry him."

"Well, ask her, Jon," Damodar entreated him. "Don't let us stop you."

"Christine, you know I've always loved you, and you're the only woman I've ever loved," Jon said intently. "No matter what happens, I'll always love you. And I would want you as my wife."

"And I say yes, Jon," she wept bitterly. "I will always say yes."

"There's your answer," Damodar spread his hands. "Consider yourselves blessed. I say unto you, before Kali you are as man and wife."

"Lakshmi, please," Christine sobbed. "If my heart hadn't gone out to you on that street, you would have never gotten in here. If you believe you have to take someone, take somebody else. Let us go, let us live our lives together, let us have children of our own. Your god can't be so cruel and heartless to demand that you kill those who've shown mercy towards you."

"You don't understand any of this, and how can I possibly explain it to you?" Lakshmi seemed regretful. "It is all predestination, this is what the gods have ordained. Kali is just one of many gods, as is Krishna and all the rest. One god cannot change the direction of all the gods. The path of all beings is ordained since before the beginning of time. We could no more have chosen not to come here than you could have avoided being here. This was your destiny, to have learned that Jon was to take you as his wife. Now you will pass on to your next incarnation together, you will be bound together forever just as Jean-Guy and I."

"You can't do this to us," Christine begged. "You can't, you can't."

"So you're telling me there's no way out," Jon mused. "Even if I told you exactly where a couple, far richer than we, lived in this same building. You couldn't change your luck and end up with someone or something better?"

"This must be done by midnight," Damodar replied. "If we do not perform the ritual by midnight we will be trapped in these bodies for the rest of their natural lives."

"I am going to bathe," Lakshmi announced. "I am going to endure the last moments of time in this wretched body in a state of cleanliness."

The three of them remained engrossed in their own thoughts as Lakshmi went to the bathroom and filled the tub. They could hear her splashing around, the sound of her bathing blending with that of the grandfather clock ticking loudly in the anteroom by the doorway.

By the time she returned, it was 11 PM. Jon realized that he had exactly one hour to change the fate prepared for him by the Great Kali.

Chapter Nine

"The time grows nearer."

"Yes, my darling."

Lakshmi had returned to the room wrapped in towels which covered the nakedness of her tiny frame. Both Jon and Christine were stricken with horror as they saw the terrible scars across her back which told of vicious beatings to a child not yet having reached her puberty. Damodar gazed upon her with a look that told them that he also bore such scars.

"Perhaps you would like to bathe as well," she took her seat on the sofa alongside him.

"In less than an hour, we will be in a situation that would make the notion ludicrous," Damodar smiled. "No, let us keep watch over our friends here so that nothing can possibly go wrong."

At once they could hear a commotion in the hall outside. Jon realized that there were guests arriving at the suite down the hall, and room service was helping them get situated.

"*Help!*" Christine screamed at the top of her lungs.

At once Damodar pulled a push dagger from his left sneaker top, drawing it from its sheath as he leapt on top of Christina. He grabbed her by the throat as he pressed the tip of the blade against her throat, drawing a pinprick of blood.

"Damodar!" Jon snarled. "Let her go! I'll kill you, you little bastard!"

"And I will kill her if she makes one more sound!" the ugly kid retorted.

"Damodar, you can't!" Lakshmi pleaded. "If you kill her we will remain like this unto death!"

"If we are captured or arrested it will make no difference!" Damodar insisted.

"Let me gag her, then," Lakshmi insisted, rushing back to the bathroom for a hand towel. "Don't be foolish, we are less than an hour away from our goal!"

She brought back the towel, which Damodar quickly shredded so as to jam one piece into Christine's mouth. He then used the other piece to tie around her neck and jaws.

"You're gonna choke her, you son of a bitch!" Jon was irate.

Suddenly there was a knock on the door, and it was as a gunshot as the room grew silent as the grave. Damodar was like a giant spider, hopping across to where Jon lay, pressing the blade against his jugular as they listened intently to the rustling outside the door.

"Room service," a voice called from the hallway. "Everything okay?"

"Believe me when I tell you this," Damodar whispered to Jon. "I believed everything you told me about your American prisons. I would rather die out on the street than be sent to one of them. I will kill you before risking capture."

"You're going to kill us anyway, you little son of a bitch," Jon twisted his neck away from the blade.

"At least I offer you the hope of reincarnation with your woman," Damodar grabbed his hair so he could not pull away. "If I kill you now you will come back as a worm!"

"Screw you, you little bastard!" Jon yelled, and Damodar jumped to his feet before placing his foot across Jon's throat. Jon was helpless as the boy's weight nearly choked him unconscious.

Once again they heard footsteps at the door, and there was a faint knock, much lighter than the first. The persons grew quiet before eventually going their way down the hall.

"So you will not go peacefully on to your next evolution," Damodar realized, heading to the bathroom for a second towel which he shredded into a gag for Jon. At 5'10" and 185, he was almost twice Damodar's size, but the boy's foot on his throat nullified the difference as he forced Jon to open his mouth to accept the knot of cloth. In short order both Christine and Jon were unable to make a sound.

"It grows late," Lakshmi looked up at the clock. "It is best that we start making our preparations."

Damodar lifted his hoodie and loosened his jeans to reveal the handle of a long jeweled ceremonial blade. Jon and Christina were taken aback at the sight, the knife appearing almost as a museum piece possibly worth thousands of dollars. They also realized that this was the instrument the kids would use for whatever their strange fantasy would require. They were both working their tongues and their jaws against their gags, but as surreptitiously as possible so as to not draw the attention of the Indian kids.

"Let us remove these two to the bathroom area so that we may work without distraction," Lakshmi suggested. Dakodar agreed, and they went first to Christine and grabbed her ankles to drag her across the carpeted floor to the bathroom area. She started struggling at first, but the threat of Damodar's foot across her throat quickly deterred her. After they dragged Christine to the bathroom door, they next returned for Jon.

He seemed docile as they grabbed him under each arm, grunting as they hoisted him off the floor and began dragging him to where Christine lay. He dropped himself into a dead weight mode, making it exceedingly difficult to haul him as they had Christine. They had gotten him halfway across the floor when, at once, he bucked and lunged violently, smashing both feet against the heavy table near the middle of the room. The table toppled and fell to the floor, with the big lamp combining to create a crashing sound.

"You damned fool! You stupid idiot!" Damodar stepped on Jon's throat to choke him out. Jon's vision began to blur under the great pressure on his windpipe when, suddenly, there was another knock on the door.

"Mr. Farrow?" the voice called, then knocked again with authority. "Mr. Farrow."

"All right, you dolt!" Damodar hissed, grabbing him by the shirt. "Listen very carefully. Charlotte will be in the bathroom with Christine. She will be holding the knife to her eye sockets. If you make one false move, she will cut her eyes right out of her head. No matter how this ends, she will live the rest of her life as a blind, deformed freak. Now I am going to untie you, and you will send the intruder away. I will be sitting right behind you on the sofa, watching and listening. Be very, very careful, Jon."

Once again Jon was tempted to throw the demonic sacrifice back in his face, but realized he was getting yet another opportunity to play for time. His mind raced as the kids dragged Christine all the way into the bathroom, Damodar giving the ceremonial dagger to Lakshmi before he returned to Jon and cut the plastic ties from his wrists and ankles.

"Remember, you clod," Damodar warned him. "If you make a mistake, your intended will pay frightfully. She will go into her next life as an eyeless freak."

Jon rubbed his wrists and smoothed his clothes before heading over to the door. He glanced over his shoulder at Damodar, sitting peacefully on the sofa. He opened the door and found Jenkins the doorman at the threshold.

"Good evening, Mr. Farrow," the elderly black man gave his toothy grin. "I most certainly did not want to disturb you, but I was helping the room service folks bring some luggage up to the Asners' suite at the end of the hall. I heard some strange noises and I wanted to make sure everything was okay."

"Why certainly, Jenkins...I mean Jeeves. I'm always getting your name wrong, and I'm glad you corrected me the other day," Jon crossed his eyes. "Say, and when you go back downstairs, be sure and tell Security Source I won't be needing them tonight, everything's just fine."

"Why, sure," the doorman seemed quizzical. "I see that little fellow you brought in seems to have settled in. I saw your lady friend had brought that little girl up with her as well."

"Yes, she's helping the little girl in the bath," Jon explained breezily. "We do volunteer work on the weekends, kinda like fostering. It really makes the holidays worthwhile."

"That certainly is true," he chuckled in agreement. "Now, if you need anything, just call the front desk. Have a blessed Christmas."

Jon closed the door and returned to Damodar, who hopped out of his seat and quickly bound Jon's wrists behind his back with another quick-lock. He then prodded him into a kneeling position before binding his ankles and pushing him to the carpet.

"Stupid bastard!' Damodar fumed. "The lackey's name was Jenkins, he already told you!"

"Well, dammit, kid, you don't exactly have me in the frame of mind for a game of Jeopardy."

"And what in hell is Security Source?" Damodar demanded.

"Christine mentioned it before, it's a security service we subscribe to. Sometimes they send someone around to check doors, things like that. People routinely call to suspend service for the evening if they don't want to be disturbed."

"Damodar!" Lakshmi called him, nodding up at the clock. The kids then grabbed Jon under each arm and dragged him to the bathroom, dropping him next to Christine.

"The time is approaching," Damodar told them. "I will loose the gag from her mouth provided she does not scream. Rest assured that if either of you tries to attract further attention I will cut your tongues out!"

"We certainly wouldn't want you to go to the Devil with your tongues missing," Jon baited him.

"Keep still, and make your peace with each other," Damodar wagged the blade at him before leaving the bathroom.

"Oh my gosh, Jon, what'll we do? That little maniac is going to kill us!" Christine's eyes remained misty.

"He'll make a mistake, he's under too much pressure," Jon reassured her. "He thinks he has until midnight to get this done. To my limited knowledge of psychiatry, even when the patient is experiencing a hallucination or undergoing a delusional episode, a severe shock or trauma will often bring them back to reality. If they actually see blood, or if I can create some sort of diversion in the middle of their ritual, it might make one or both of them snap."

"What do you mean, see blood?" she trembled.

"If worse comes to worse, I'll see to it that they start with me," he replied. "If part of their delusion is that needs to get done at midnight, they'll want to choose a path of least resistance, which would mean taking out the main resister."

"Jon, don't talk like that, I'm scared to death!" she pleaded.

"We've still got time to think, there must be a way," Jon assured her.

In the next room, Damodar found Christmas ornaments that included some large, thick holiday candles. He cut the candles into twelve pieces and carefully placed them in the shape of a pentagram on the carpet. He then produced a tiny amulet from beneath his shirt, which was the sign of the Great Kali. The triple-headed demon had one eye in each of its heads and necks as those of snakes, which adjoined to ape-like shoulders and a chest perched upon a gargantuan belly. Four legs provided the lap upon which the monstrous weight rested.

Damodar next stripped himself naked, wrapping his loins in a towel as had Lakshmi. They lit the candles and joined hands as they began to pray to the great demon. Almost as if by magic, the electricity began to dim and the air in the room began to thin as the supernatural presence of Kali began to make itself known.

"Christine," Jon stared into her eyes, "I have a very important question to ask you."

"What?" she asked, tears streaming down her cheeks.

"Have you ever accepted Jesus Christ as your personal Savior?"

"*What?*" she stared in disbelief.

"Look, just in case things don't work out for us," Jon said. "You know we've never really taken time to stop and smell the roses together. We've never stopped what we were doing to discuss a lot of things, the things that really matter. I love you, Christine, and I don't think I've ever told anyone else that, or felt about them the way I feel about you. And if there is a hereafter, I wouldn't want to think we weren't going there together, or if one of us was going somewhere different. Maybe those two misguided little wretches out there are going to their own private hell, but I want to know we're both going to a better place together."

"Jon, this is crazy," she gasped. "Those little monsters are planning to kill us, and you're carrying on like some televangelist!"

"Please, Christine," he pleaded. "Just bear with me. Listen to your heart for a minute. This whole Christmas thing is about Jesus Christ. Forget the holiday trees, the decorations, Santa Claus, the presents and all the other crap. It's about this man whose birth and death they celebrate like no one else's. There's got to be something behind it, and this is going to be like taking out collision insurance when we rent a car. These little cretins may not kill us, but if they do, at least we're covered."

"They can't kill us, they can't!" she wept.

"Baby, please answer me. Do you accept Christ as your personal Savior?"

"Yes, yes, I do," she cried. "Just don't let them kill us."

"Okay, let's close our eyes and pray together," Jon entreated her. "We'll ask for His help, and then we'll just let go and let God."

Meanwhile, down in the lobby, Rufus Jenkins was doing some soul-searching of his own. He was somewhat miffed that Jon Farrow had gotten his name wrong again in such a short time. At first he tried to blow off the perceived insult, but there was something about it that was out of sync. He couldn't figure why Farrow crossed his eyes either. Perhaps it was an idiosyncrasy, the way people made funny faces when they did something out of sorts. He did ask that his security service be called off for the evening, and that was very odd as he should have been able to call them himself.

As an afterthought, he contacted the security desk and asked them about Jon Farrow's security arrangement. He was given the number of Security Source and decided to give them a call.

Jenkins gave them the message that the service was not needed this evening, and the customer service rep asked him to hold for a supervisor.

"Thank you for holding. This is Captain Shreve."

Once again Jenkins told what had happened in relaying the message.

"Thank you very much for calling us," Shreve said tautly. "Do you work for the hotel?"

"Yes sir."

"We would appreciate it if you can notify hotel security to keep an eye on that floor and that suite and let us know if anyone comes in or out," he was instructed. "We'd prefer that you allow us to make contact with the authorities if necessary in order to protect the privacy of our client. We'll have one of our people over to follow up as soon as possible."

Jenkins hung up, hoping that he had not done anything to inconvenience the Christmas Eve celebration of Jon Farrow, his beautiful girlfriend, and the lucky waifs they had brought home in such a magnaminous gesture.

Chapter Ten

"Now is the time."

"Yes, let us begin," Lakshmi said encouragingly.

They proceeded to the bathroom where they first hauled Christine out by the ankles, dragging her back into the living room before pulling Jon out by both arms. The couple was startled by the appearance of the candles in the middle of the carpet set in the shape of the pentagram. It fleetingly crossed Jon's mind how much damage the melting wax would have done to the expensive flooring.

Damodar had set one of Jon's briefcases in the middle of the pentagram to be used as an altar of sorts. He set the ceremonial dagger in the middle of the briefcase and set four burning chunks of candle on each of its four corners. He then knelt alongside the makeshift altar and began muttering arcane incantations in order to conjure up the spirit of the Great Kali.

"Jon, it's starting," Christine whispered, not wanting to incur the wrath of the worshippers by interrupting their demonic rite. "What are we going to do?"

"You keep praying," Jon implored her. "I'm still thinking."

Lakshmi closed her eyes and joined in the diabolical chant, and at once she began spasming and writhing as a demon began to take possession of her body, Her eyes began rolling in her head as she foamed at the mouth, her body arching backward as Jon and Christine watched in amazement. Damodar was also shaking as if someone seized by an epileptic fit, yet he was able to remain in place as he continued to offer prayers to Kali.

"Kali, destroyer of time, god of skeletal form, taking the form of a raven, blacker than black, I worship you, O Daksina Kalika!" Damodar gasped as he stared unseeing towards the ceiling.

At once Jon and Christine felt the hairs on their bodies standing as if affected by an electrical charge. The room seemed to drop in temperature as an unearthly atmosphere began overwhelming the suite.

"I bow to you, Kalika, Maharaudri, fond of the night, Devi liking kunda, gola and svayambhu flowers!" Lakshmi began to wail. "Those who pronounce the mantra Krim Hrim Hrum Svaha seven times over the cremation pyre, then encircle the houses of their enemies with the ashes shall destroy their enemies!"

"If they go any deeper into this trance, I'm going to roll towards the door and start kicking against it. I'm pretty sure that someone will complain, and they'll probably call the front desk. If Jenkins made mention of coming by and checking on us, it's almost sure to create suspicion. Let's just give this a few more seconds and see how tight they get wound up," Jon said intently, staring at the convulsing youngsters.

"Kalika, of terrible form, who bestows the fruit of all desires, the Devi praised by all gods, destroy all my enemies!" Damodar grabbed the dagger in both hands and raised it towards the ceiling. "Om, true form of Hrim, hram, Hrim and hrum, true form of hram Hrim ksaim ksaum, kill my enemies!"

Just as Damodar prepared for the sacrifice to begin, he had no way of knowing that the Security Source patrol car had just pulled up outside the Plaza residences. Jenkins came over to him and explained the situation in detail, giving Captain Shreve the room number and verifying the code to the door lock which he already had on file. Shreve thanked him and began filling out his activity report before going up to investigate.

Damodar and Lakshmi recovered from their trances sufficiently to come over to Christine and drag her before the makeshift altar, She begged and pleaded with them to no avail as Lakshmi stood over her, going back into her trance as she continued to call upon Kali.

"Oh, Lord Jesus, please have mercy on my soul!" Christine cried out.

"Wait!" Damodar stopped short as if a glass of cold water had been thrown in his face. "Is this a Christian?"

"It cannot be!" Lakshmi also began coming out of her trance. "She is a money worshiper!"

Let not a practitioner of the mystic rite use the blood of a Christian in his ritual, nor the Christian grave as a place of sacrifice, lest the wrath of Hell be brought from the depths against him.

—The Rituals of Diabolus

"No, it mustn't be!" Damodar broke into a cold sweat as he looked up at the clock showing the time as a quarter to midnight. "There is no time to make a change!"

"Then go without me, my love!" Lakshmi began to weep. "Sacrifice the un-believing man to Kali and assume his being. Somehow we will meet again!"

"No!" Damodar cried out in anguish. "I will never leave you nor forsake you!"

At once Jon exploded in a paroxysm of adrenaline-charged fury. The indignity of what was happening to them, combined with his anger and shame over not being able to protect and defend Christine, placed him in a state of temporary insanity. He was as a man watching his wife trapped under a burning vehicle, possessed by such anxiety that he was able to snap the quick-lock on his ankles with the strength of a madman.

"Look!" Lakshmi stared in astonishment. "The man has broken free!"

Jon leaped to his feet and lunged at Lakshmi, kicking her as hard as he could in the midsection as if punting a football. He lifted her off the ground with the force of the kick, sending her flying through the air across the room where she smashed into the small table by the window. He then charged wildly into Damodar, bashing him with a shoulder tackle though his hands remained tied behind his back. The scrawny kid went flying into the table heaped with presents, sending it crashing across the carpet as he sprawled onto the floor.

"Christina, the door!" Jon yelled. "Roll over to the door! Start kicking on the door!" He next ran over to Lakshmi and gave her a vicious kick to the ribs as she tried to regain her feet. He then ran to Damodar, who had rolled to his knees and brought forth his push dagger.

"All right, it's over," Damodar wheezed from the effects of the shoulder block, brandishing the blade as he stumbled to his feet. "Let us leave now, we have failed in our quest."

"You little son of a bitch, you wanted to kill me, go for it!" Jon yelled at him, straining at the quick-lock binding his wrists.

And all the devils besought him, saying, Send us into the swine, that we may enter into them. And forthwith Jesus gave them leave. And the unclean spirits went out, and entered into the swine.

—the Gospel of Mark

Christine had rolled over to the door and began kicking against it with all her might. It was just as Captain Shreve reached the front door, and he quickly punched in the codes and shoved it open. Only Christine was lying at the threshold and blocked him from coming in.

"Security!" Shreve announced. "This is security, open the door!"

At that very moment, the new tenants of the suite down the hall had just arrived after a theatre event and a late dinner. Mr. and Mrs. Edmond Asner were multimedia billionaires, having inherited their fortunes and amassed great wealth over their lifetimes. Constance Asner was known as a glutton and a lover of money, and Edmond was an unscrupulous man who had destroyed his rivals and cared nothing for the lives of those he cast aside in his quest for money and power. They had bought the condo so as to have a place to stay for the holidays, planning to return to their mansion in Key Largo afterwards for the remainder of the winter season.

Damodar threw the knife at Jon and grabbed Lakshmi by the hand. Lifting her from the floor, he threw open the glass door to the balcony and pulled her outside. Christine had rolled away from the door and Captain Shreve rushed into the room, producing a Swiss knife from his pocket so as to cut her loose from her bonds. Jon watched with mixed emotions that gave way to alarm as the two kids climbed onto the balcony rail.

"No! Don't!" Jon called to them. "I'll help you, don't do this!"

They looked back at him and gave him a wistful smile before they jumped, holding hands as they fell twelve stories to the pavement. Their tiny bodies exploded as watermelons upon impact, drenching the Asners at curbside with their blood. The Asners staggered back in shock, and the bystanders gazing in horror at the gruesome scene did not notice the elderly couple going into spasms as the spirits of Jean-Guy Perrault and Charlotte Dupree took possession of their bodies.

"Holy crap!" Shreve ran to cut Jon loose as Christine crawled weeping to the sofa. "This place is a wreck! What the hell happened?"

"Those kids we brought up here pulled knives on us," Jon said numbly, visibly shaken by the sight of the children jumping to their deaths. "They had a knife at Christine's throat in the bathroom when Jenkins came up earlier. When you came in they jumped off the balcony."

"My god," Shreve exclaimed, rushing onto the balcony, looking down to where a crowd had gathered around the unrecognizable little corpses. The Asners had already been ushered into the building where they were being attended to by the hotel staff. "I'll go ahead and fill out my report, but I'm sure the police will be here any minute."

"Oh, Jon," Christine rushed over to him, throwing herself into his arms, "I've never been so scared in all my life!"

"It's okay now, baby," he held her close, and could not help but add, "your faith has saved us."

They could hear the sirens wailing down below, and Jon went over and picked up the velvet box from the carpet where it had been knocked off the table. He silently gave it to Christine, who began sobbing as she took the diamond ring from the box and slipped it onto her finger.

Jon peered out through the open door and could see Jenkins and a couple of bellhops escorting the Asners to their suite down the hall. The elderly couple's evening wear was stained with blood, but they seemed quite serene as they were led to their room. As they passed, Edmond Asner looked directly at Jon, staring into his eyes before giving him a knowing smile.

"I'm just so sorry that something like this happened," Shreve lamented as the police arrived at the door. "I only wish I could've gotten here earlier. It couldn't have happened at a worse time of the year."

"Jon Farrow?" the officer in charge came over. "Do you live here? Is this your condo?"

"Not for much longer," Jon replied numbly.

He intended to put as much distance between himself, the spirits of Jean-Guy Perrault and Charlotte Dupree, and Edmond and Constance Asner as soon as humanly possible

Chapter Eleven

Edd

Max Bridgman was considered the biggest up and coming star in the publicity world. He had worked with some of the newest stars in the entertainment business and was now dabbling in the political field. His multimedia strategies were considered upbeat, innovative, and provided segues for his clients to launch their promotional campaigns with an eclectic panache. He was now earning $500K per year and was close to realizing his dream of financial security for life. He had bought his dream home in New Braunfels, Texas on a hundred acres of land and even had his own stable. His fantasies were becoming reality at last, but his biggest concern was being able to have time to smell the roses in the wonderful world he was creating for himself.

Some of his newer clients had grown almost paranoid in the turbulent political climate in the Lone Star State, and Max was nearly on-call for some of them as they approached their campaign launch dates. They wanted to make sure their messages were motivational and upbeat, their posters and flyers inspiring and catchy, and the slogans neither ambivalent nor contradictory to any central theme. Dirty politics were such that no one wanted to bring anything to the table that could be rubbed in their faces or held up as a rebuke and disgrace as their campaigns closed in on voting deadlines.

One of his favorite memories from his days at UTSA was in a public speaking class where the professor did a lecture on "We The People". He had the class write a one-page composition on it during class, then emphasized all three words and analyzed the different implications of each. WE the people might suggest elitism to critics, while We THE people could imply a specificity, and

We the PEOPLE conjured up notions of proletarianism. It ignited a strong debate within the classroom, and Max never forgot how emphasis on a single word was like a spark that could start a forest fire.

Political correctness was taking all the vim and vigor out of the business, and it seemed his job was all about preventing fires than igniting the flames of inspiration among voters. The politicians were so worried about having a Teflon-coated public image that they let nothing stick, not even reputations for quality and character. It was as if they would rather be remembered for nothing wrong rather than anything right that could be used against them. It was boring and hypocritical in his mind, but the customer was always right. He would simply go about his business in establishing Mr. Nobodies, though he wished someone would one day step up to the plate and dare be Mr. Somebody.

He wanted to hitch his wagon to one particular star, get that magical call from the Next American Hero who would appear as a shining star on the political horizon. He wanted to see someone who would stand on the Constitution in re-establishing America's fundamental rights and principles, redefine the USA as the light of the world, bring an end to the Great Recession, and cure the common cold. Although his personal dreams might soon become reality, his political fantasies might very well remain just that.

And so it was that Max would take time off to wander off and indulge in dreams.

He had scheduled this particular weekend to commune with nature and seek harmony with his inner self. He chose the Hill Country for its scenic beauty, as close to the Wild West fantasies of his youth as he ever expected to get. He let his mare Sugar get her head, galloping up and down the hills as she saw fit. He loved his horse, loved her sense of perception, her way of understanding him as if she could read his mind. Getting out with her like this was cathartic, a way for her to let herself free and letting him share the experience. She ran and ran until she got tired, and he got off so she could blow and snort and cool herself off. He hugged her jawbone and patted her cheek, looping her rein around a bush as he walked around to stretch his legs.

As they continued to ride along, he saw what appeared to be an abandoned farmhouse in the distance that somehow appeared to be recently vacated. There appeared to be fresh hay near the barn that had not been pitched, and a few sacks of fertilizer that appeared to have recently delivered. Yet there were no fresh tracks, human or otherwise, and the windows were so dusty that the house seemed uninhabited. The last thing he wanted to do was to appear to be trespassing, but he was interested in acquiring property in this area and wanted to inquire.

Help me.

It was almost as if someone had whispered loudly into his ear, as if the Central Texas wind had bunched itself into a cluster and exploded against the side of his head. It would have been unmistakable had it not carried the impact of a hot gust of air that easily played tricks on the mind in this kind of heat. He remembered when he first stepped off the plane at Austin International Airport ten years ago and that same wind hit him like a blast from a furnace. First impressions lasted a lifetime, especially those made by the kind of air that introduced itself before it hit you.

"Hello, the house," he called loudly, not remembering where he had heard such a corny line. It might have come from one of those Zane Gray novels he had absorbed as a teenager in Chicago, the kind of books that drove him to Texas to become an urban cowboy. Back home, walking around in a cowboy hat and boots, Western shirt and jeans could have had one mistaken for a midnight cowboy. Here in Texas, he was dressed in the height of fashion. Only at times like this, he wished he could have had a six-gun strapped to his hip.

Help me.

This time the sound made his spine tingle, a chill sweeping over his body. It was a disembodied voice without sound, having neither accent nor timbre, nothing identifiable but the spoken words. If Moses indeed heard a voice speaking to him from the burning bush at Mt. Sinai, it must have been a voice such as this. Though he was not what he considered a religious man, he did give credence to the supernatural as something beyond the six senses. There had been too much cumulative evidence over the centuries suggesting the existence of a fourth dimension, a time/space warp that even Einstein recognized. He just hoped that whatever was attached to this voice was something he could deal with.

He ground-tethered Sugar before getting down and stretching his legs, looking around to gain his bearings. There was no sign of man or beast, and he realized it was highly likely that he was hearing things. He knew that it was going to be a scorcher, over a hundred degrees for the second week in a row, and he would have to change clothes as soon as he got home. He knew that he was somewhat of a neat freak, not to mention a control freak and obsessive-compulsive to a minor fault. He lost his marriage over it, but he was taking steps to get it all back. As a matter of fact, he was going to get hard to work on it as soon as he returned home.

Kay Aniston was one of the most beautiful women he had ever met. She was a bit of a social climber, her family of the *nouveau riche* elite. They were those who lied, cheated and stole their way to the top and held those who did not survive the climb in contempt. He loved her dearly but often grew physically ill when she tore down their neighbors and acquaintances, comparing them to her family who could never do wrong in her eyes. She planned more and more of their leisure time with her relatives, and the more he tried to withdraw, the greater the rift between them grew. It cost them their marriage, but she was starting to see things differently now that his absence was making her heart grow fonder.

Help me.

He made his way to the barn, painfully aware that here in Texas this could get you shot. He could see that the tattered shades had been drawn at each dust-coated window. It was entirely possible that the house was used sparingly, if at all. Its owner might have been a livestock trader who used the place for stopovers in driving across the great state of Texas, which was a day's journey from Houston to El Paso or Dalhart to Corpus Christi.

He stepped around the side of the barn and saw a grayish underweight horse that seemed to have been abandoned by its owner with a bale of moldy hay and a moss-covered trough of water to relieve its thirst. His sense of righteous indignation immediately came to the fore, and he was hoping that someone came across him so he could give them a good tongue-lashing for mistreating this poor horse. He went over and patted it, then mechanically untied its tether so as to let it walk and stretch its legs. Max did not doubt that the horse had probably been standing in the same place for days on end.

"Well, fellow," Max caressed his face, "I think I'm gonna take you for a nice walk. I'll leave a note in the door and tell your owner where to find you. And if he has a problem with that, I've got quite a few friends who'll be glad to tie a knot in his tail when they hear about this."

He brought the horse out to the front of the property, tethering its rein to the back of Sugar's saddle before pulling a pen and paper out of his saddlebag. He tried using his cell phone but, as always, he was unable to get a signal out here. He wrote a curt note indicating he had come to the house in search of directions and came across the horse in a state of neglect. He put his phone number on the note along with that of his attorney in case he was unavailable. If these people did not really want the horse anymore, the lawyer's number would have been enough to discourage a callback.

"Okay, boy," Max said as he mounted Sugar, "We're gonna take you along for a good meal, clean water to drink and a nice place to sleep. I don't know if these folks are gonna call to come claim you, but they sure will catch hell when they do."

He had rode about ten miles in this direction, and headed back along the same farm road from whence they came. Most of the traffic along the hillside was pickup trucks, beat-up antiques used as alternative means of transportation, or teenagers out running their motors past the speed limit. As a result, there were lots of dead deer, skunks, coyotes and armadillos lining the sides of the road, and animal lovers such as himself would have been knee-deep in people's crap had he chosen a career in law enforcement. He was often disheartened by the fact that society had grown so materialistic and cynical that people could no longer appreciate the simple pleasures in life that nature provided. He wondered why they would choose to live in a place like Texas with that screwed-up attitude.

They returned to his spacious ranch house, where he brought the horses back out to the barnyard and stable area. The stable contained six stalls, which was greatly convenient as Max could put Sugar in a clean stall while he cleaned out her used one. He had a good deal going with one of his neighbors, who would pick up the sacks of horse manure in exchange for fresh oats and hay. It was kind of like exchanging what came out of one end for what went in the other. He knew that horse manure was great for fertilizer, and he figured his neighbor had an arrangement made for what Sugar contributed to the local ecology.

He put the horses in adjoining stalls and made sure they had a fresh bale of hay and plenty of water before removing Sugar's saddle and bringing it back to the barn. He figured he would come out tomorrow morning and give both horses a good brushing. He had some work to do for Representative Schneider's upcoming campaign for re-election, and would spend the rest of the day and evening on it after calling Kay.

She always kept her answering machine running so she could screen calls. She was one of those who disliked chatting on the phone, and took calls only when it was someone she wanted or needed to talk to. Right after the divorce, it was like calling the White House, but over the past few weeks she would pick up and interrupt his message.

"Hello? Max?" she jumped in before he got through his first sentence.

"Hi, pretty girl," his heart seemed to skip a beat when he talked to her on the phone these days. Regardless of their differences, he had never stopped loving her. "I just got back from riding Sugar. You'll never guess what happened."

"Don't tell me. You picked up a family of stray armadillos."

"Not exactly. I rescued a neglected horse." He then went on to tell her the story of how he found the horse and brought him home.

"Oh, Max, I can't believe you did that," Kay was upset. "You know there are still laws on the books here in Texas for stealing horses? You had better call Baron Saunders immediately and tell him what you did."

"Okay, okay," he relented, considering that it might be wise to get some advice from his lawyer in this situation. "Listen, I may be incommunicado for the rest of the day. I've got to get to work on Dennis' campaign, and it'll probably keep me busy until bedtime. I just wanted to call and touch bases."

"Well, that's sweet of you. Just be sure and call Baron. I don't want to be worried about them sending the sheriff after you."

"Will do, baby. Talk to you later."

Max next phoned Baron Saunders, a long-time family friend who ironically had been the one handling their divorce proceeding. Baron had his 'away from his desk' message going but responded just before Max hung up. They exchanged friendly greetings before Max explained the situation in detail.

"I don't know, Max, this can get kinda hairy," Baron cautioned him. "If the horse's owner gets their dander up, this can get messy. He can file criminal charges for criminal trespass and horse theft. On the other hand, if you came upon the property asking for directions, came across an abandoned animal and left a note, that somewhat eliminates any criminal intent. I'll tell you what, let me get the sheriff out there and have him file a report. That will at least cover our bases provided the owner hasn't called first."

Max went back inside and got to work on Dennis' account. Schneider was a libertarian who had a considerable Tea Party following due to his strong platform on privacy issues and his lobbying against the Administration's policies of Internet surveillance and political persecution of opposition groups. The Tea Party had been irked by recent allegations against the IRS for auditing organizations and denying their tax exemptions for rallying support against abortion and racial profiling. Schneider was a highly vocal antagonist whose campaign slogan was, "We Will Be Heard". No matter which word was emphasized, the message was clear enough.

The only call that came through was from the Travis County Sheriff's Department, advising him that they did find the property to appear deserted and that they would take steps to contact the owner. The fact that Max had documentation of Coggins (*equine infectious anemia) testing for Sugar proved he was a responsible horse owner, and they saw no reason why he could not shelter the horse until the owner was located or the animal was claimed.

Max stayed up until 10 PM working on the campaign proposals and strategies, then finally decided to call it a night. He would be driving up to Austin to meet with Schneider on Monday and wanted to make sure that Dennis was comfortable with the program. He only hoped he wouldn't be asked to stay over as the campaign got underway in case any damage control was necessary. He thought that was the most ludicrous part of the job, but didn't mind getting the travel accommodations when there was no way around it.

When he woke up the next morning, he went out to the stable and got one of the worst shocks of his life. He found the new horse munching happily on his oats, looking much better than he did in the abandoned barn yesterday. He came over to Sugar's stall and found her lying on her side, shivering and blowing with extreme difficulty. There was traces of blood in the mucus leaking from her nose, causing Max to race back to the house to call the vet.

Dr. Altchek came out to the ranch as quickly as he could, and gave Sugar what Max thought was a cursory check-up before confronting him with great concern.

"My god, Max, I think the animal has anthrax," he was unnerved. "I'm going to have to notify the Sheriff's Office and the Board of Health. This horse is too far gone, it'll have to be put down. They'll also have to burn the carcass to prevent the disease from spreading."

"Good lord, Sal," Max broke into tears. "She was just fine yesterday. Do you think she caught it from the other horse?"

"He appears to be in fine shape, but if you can bring him up to the house away from the other one I'll run some tests," Altchek replied. "I'm terribly sorry about this, but the law requires that I notify the Board of Health..."

"Don't worry, Doc, I know this is a bad situation," Max wiped her eyes. "I'll bring the other horse up to the house."

He trudged across the yard with the horse in tow, leading him by the rein on his bridle as he stared through misty eyes at Sugar, already in her death throes. He had the mare since she was a colt, and it sickened him to be losing her so abruptly to such a horrible illness. He was somewhat glad that the inspectors would be by to give the property a clean bill of health. It was terrible that he got this new horse under such awful conditions, but he was determined that he was going to be very happy in this new home.

"I guess it's just you and me, fellow," Max said as he tied the reins to the old-fashioned hitching post he had in front of the house.

Just you and me.

He was almost startled by the hot Texas wind that whistled past, sounding almost as if someone had whispered in his ear. He looked at the horse and laughed at himself, glad to have something to lighten the atmosphere however momentarily. Max patted the horse and went inside, preparing himself before calling Kay to have a shoulder to cry on.

Chapter Twelve

"So you're telling me you couldn't reach anyone on your cell phone. Max, how on earth do people out in the Hill Country communicate without cell phones?"

"I didn't say it was impossible for people to get signals out there, I just said my service doesn't seem to work out there. Otherwise I would've called the sheriff," Max insisted. Kay always seemed to think that whatever went down, it had to be a byproduct of his negligence.

"Well, what are you going to do with that sick horse?" she inquired as they debated the issue over the phone the next morning. The health inspector had come out and taken samples, asking that he keep the area off-limits until their reports came back from their laboratory. To Max's benefit, the Animal Control people had come out and picked up Sugar's carcass and disposed of it according to procedure. They were not forced to euthanize her as she was dead by the time they arrived.

"I already told you what happened to her," Max was nettled.

"I'm talking about that beast you rescued."

"Who, Edd? He's fine, he just needed a little care and attention. He's a completely different horse now."

"Ed? Why did you give him a name like that?"

"That's his name," Max managed. "Listen, hon, I've got to go. I need to call Dennis and get my schedule for this week. I'll give you a call tonight."

He really didn't feel as if he needed any further distractions at this point in time, but there was something very strange going on with Edd that he was going to have to get a grip on once this situation with Dennis Schneider was resolved.

The horse was communicating with him somehow. He wasn't sure if it was his mind playing tricks on him, or if it was some strange form of telepathy. He couldn't rule out the possibility that the Government, or some private firm, might have come up with some experimental project allowing them to manipulate brain waves. Perhaps even some occult society had come up with some arcane spell that could cause people to hallucinate, believing that they were hearing voices from unusual sources.

"I wonder what we're gonna call you?" Jon was shoveling oats from a storage bin into a sack he would dump into the horse's feeder. It was the night before as Sugar lay dying, and he had brought the horse into the garage where he had set up provisions for Sugar in case the stables were unavailable.

My name is Edd.

He knew that sometimes people got giddy bordering on euphoric after a short period of exertion, similar to athletes coming off the field after a successful undertaking. He even considered the fact that it might have been some strange coincidence as the sun and the horseback ride played tricks on his mind when he first heard a voice call to him that afternoon. Regardless, he had worked up a sweat and was trying to catch his breath, and just played along with himself.

"Sure, Ed, welcome to the crazy house," he chuckled, wiping his brow. He had not installed an air conditioner in the garage, and it was hot as hell in there.

That's Edd with two D's.

"Wait a second. What in hell is going on here? You're not trying to talk to me, are you? Am I losing my friggin' mind?"

That appeared to have been the end of the episode as the horse went incommunicado. He put Edd on a long tether and left the garage door open so the night breeze could cool the place out, and the horse could walk outside as far as the threshold in case he wanted a more comfortable place to stand.

After Kay had hung up, he began surfing the Internet to learn more about hearing voices and hallucinations. He knew it might well have been caused by heat exposure, and he realized that every time he thought he heard voices he had been exposed to heat well around the ninety-degree mark. Plus he had been in various stages of physical exertion. Rather than bringing this to a doctor's attention and risk having the Government adding such information to his medical records, he decided to blow off the incidents and install air conditioning in the garage as a precaution.

He decided to give Dennis a call to figure out what would be the next step in their game plan. The current Administration's plan to monitor Internet activity in an effort to thwart domestic terrorism was creating a firestorm. Dennis Schneider was adamantly opposed to it and catching flak from hardcore right-wing groups. The latest IRS scandal revealing a government plot to persecute rival conservative groups was putting him directly in the middle of a crossfire. Max realized his best chance was to either build a firewall between the issues or find a defense versatile enough to cover both issues in a consolidated effort.

It seemed obvious that the solution to both issues would be greater transparency in government. If this Administration continued to obfuscate their invasions of privacy and use of inordinate leverage against opposition groups, then Schneider's people would do well to promise to be straightforward and fully accessible if they were elected to office. Identifying the groups they were opposed to and providing details as to how they were attacking them would be an ideal focus point in getting this phase of the campaign underway.

A major concern was with the White Christian Soldiers, an activist group operating out of Austin that was rapidly gaining followers throughout the South and the Northwest. Mirroring their grand strategy against that of the National Front in Great Britain, they advertised themselves as pro-white, anti-immigration Constitutionalists championing traditional American society and culture. They were at the forefront of a reactionary backlash against moderates like Schneider who were inadvertently trying to protect the rights of foreign nationals with ties to Islamic and extremist groups.

It was the increase of what he felt was the true 'graying of America' that was train-wrecking American politics. Campaigners were so caught up with political correctness, diversity and inclusivity that they were less concerned with standing firm on one point than they were in covering all bases. Schneider had become a vociferous opponent of Internet spying, but would now be at risk of losing some of the major supporters of citizens' Constitutional rights.

"So what they hell am I supposed to do, Max?" Dennis was exasperated when Max confronted him with a worst-case scenario over the phone that evening. "They're trying to put me over a barrel. Don't these knuckleheads realize that if they split the conservative vote over this privacy issue, the socialists are gonna dive right in and rake all the leftovers from the table just like last time. Everybody's in accord over the political profiling issue, can't we come to some kind of agreement over the Internet spying?"

"Dennis, I'm a spin doctor, I don't have a whole lot to do with negotiations," Max was apologetic. "I would think you might want to send a couple of your people over to WCS and have a little powwow. After all, they haven't stepped very far away from the Klan or the skinheads. One would think it'd be to their benefit to get some love from a few of the mainstream groups for some wider recognition."

"Those people are nothing but coneheads dressed in suits instead of bedsheets," Dennis was derisive. "You know, I've got an office full of volunteers, mostly retired hippies from the Sixties and college kids trying to get some references for their resumes. There's no way in hell they're gonna march into WCS Headquarters to try and broker a deal with those cross-burners. I'll tell you what just might work, and you'd be doing me a helluva favor in the process."

"Oh, no, c'mon," Max whined.

"Look, you're gonna be in town anyway. I'll tell them our publicist is trying to get more information about the group to see if there's any way we can find common ground to stand on. You're one of the best talkers I know, and you've got a better head for politics than most of the people over there on Congress Avenue. I'm sure that if you at least got to talk to these people you might be able to help me break the walls down."

"Dennis, I've got some personal issues going on here that I'm trying to resolve. I don't think this is the best time to go balls to the wall with a bunch of white activists. I had the Board of Health out here testing my property for anthrax yesterday."

"My god, Max," Dennis was concerned. "You don't suppose you stirred up any hornet's nests with one of your other clients? You know that extremists have been attacking elected officials with anthrax germs through the mail since 9/11."

"No, no, I don't think that's the case," his mind was racing. "I was specializing in the entertainment industry before I started taking on political clients. I've only had one or two, and there was nothing that could have had any kind of repercussions of that nature. I'm sure the Sheriff's Office'd be looking into it if anything looked suspicious."

"Well, I'd be careful. I just don't think these WCS people would make moves like that, especially with them trying to get some stage time under the lights."

"All right," Max relented. He knew that Dennis was going to tug at this every which way but loose, and was not going to take no for an answer. "I'll see you tomorrow morning and see what we can work out."

After he hung up, he tried to rationalize what he would probably end up doing for Schneider in Austin tomorrow. They had agreed on a $100 per day flat fee, so this would make up for a few of the days Max had billed him for a couple hours of paperwork. He decided he would approach this like an interview, and bring up a couple of Dennis' talking points in closing to see where the conversation would drift. There was a way around everything, and spin doctors were pretty good at finding them.

He was somewhat annoyed at the doorbell at this time of night, and could not think of who would be coming out here at this time of night. It was just past 9 PM and the sun was setting, and he was pretty far out in the Hill Country so it was unlikely someone would be coming by for directions. It might have been one of the neighbors, and though he kept to himself most of the time, he was always available for fencepost chats whenever someone drove by and decided to stop and visit. He got along great with all of the people he knew in the community and was not about to offend by ignoring the doorbell.

"Hey, stranger, I was in the neighborhood and thought I'd stop by," Kay smiled, standing in the doorway wearing a Mexican sun dress along with a big straw hat. The dress was one of his glaring weaknesses, and she probably remembered it from the early days of their relationship.

"Gee, I wish you'd called," Max stepped aside to allow her access. "I was just getting ready to crash out. I'm driving up to Austin first thing in the morning."

"Couldn't get out of it, huh?" she frowned. "You know, I went out to see Ed. He looks like he's in pretty good shape. I thought you said he was gray, he looks off-white to me. You got him cleaned up nice, he doesn't look much like an abused animal to me."

"It's spelled Edd with two D's," he pointed out, wondering why he did as soon as the words left his mouth. "Maybe it's the moonlight, he is a light gray. I should know, I was out there shoveling his oats and fetching his water and pitching hay for almost an hour."

"You've never been one for colors, darling," she chided him. He noticed she was wearing white sandals with pearl trim, and she had painted her toenails a pearly white. Maybe the nail polish had skewed her color perception. Once again he was feeling an unwanted stirring in his loins. "It took me a couple of years before I could get you to comprehend what teal was all about."

"I beg to differ, love, but the horse is light gray and I haven't had a chance to brush him down. I'm going to be pampering him all day Tuesday when I get back from Austin."

"Well, it's a good thing someone around here gets pampered," she exhaled, turning her heel to inspect her sandal. She had some of the loveliest legs he had ever seen, and they seemed to ripen with age as they grew fleshier and more seductive over the years. He remembered how hot she looked when they used to drive to Mustang Island on the Gulf Coast when they first met, and imagined what she would be like in a bikini right now. "You know, there was an insect out there, probably a horsefly, and I think he took a bite out of me. I thought there was a bite on my leg, but I don't see one. Can you check to see if he bit me on the back?"

"Sure, sure," he walked over as she turned her back to him. She was wearing his favorite Giorgio perfume, and being this close to her marvelous buttocks was intoxicating. She just stood there waiting, and the next thing he knew he had reached past her arms and took two handfuls of her perky breasts.

"Oh," she gasped passionately. "Oh, Max!"

It was more than he could bear, and he spun her around and slipped his tongue between her parted lips, lowering her in his arms to the carpeted floor.

She was up before dawn as usual, and he saw her touching up her makeup after emerging from the shower. The smell of her freshly scrubbed body roused him once again, but he knew she never relented in the morning and probably never would. He called her over anyway, hoping to pull that summer dress off one more time, but instead he got a kiss on the lips before she was off and running.

He started bracing himself for the hour drive to Austin, and decided to check on Edd before showering and shaving. He looked out the picture window affording him a splendid view of the Hill Country, seeing the horse standing proud in front of his temporary shelter. He smiled as he went out to greet him, planning to give him a hug and an apple before going about his business.

Better check on Dennis.

"What in the hell?" Max was dumbfounded. There was no summer breeze this morning, Kay had rejected him, and he had not lifted anything heavier than his slippers thus far. There was not a damn thing that could have explained the sound that went off in his head.

"Are you talking to me?"

91

Check on Dennis.

"Look, Edd, we really need to get a grip on this," Max broke into a cold sweat, seriously concerned about his state of mental health.

Dennis.

At once Max was overcome with a compulsion to get back to the house to see if Dennis was going to cancel their meeting. It would have been a major waste of time for him to drive all the way up there and find out something had come up, causing Dennis to reschedule.

"Max?" Mrs. Schneider answered the phone with a husky voice.

"Sylvia. How's it going?"

"Did you get my messages?"

"No, I'm sorry, Kay stayed over last night, I had the ringer off. That's why I called, I just wanted to make sure we were good to go before I took off."

"I started having migraines last night before we went to bed and I was out of hydrocodone," her voice began cracking. "Dennis called the on-call pharmacist and arranged to go down and pick it up for me. He didn't even get a mile from the house."

"Sylvia," Max's hand began trembling with apprehension. "What happened?"

"There was a hit-and-run driver, he drove off and left Dennis unconscious with the car in the middle of the intersection. No one called an ambulance until almost a half hour had passed, and by then it was too late," she began sobbing.

After Sylvia hung up, Max sat down on the recliner trying to piece it all together. The very last thing on his mind was the voices in his head which had gone silent...

...for now.

Chapter Thirteen

Max called Kay immediately after hearing the news, and she came over right away, Max was greatly distracted, mostly over the death of a close associate but also due to the fact that his entire work schedule became a casualty in the car wreck. He had devoted himself exclusively to Schneider's account and would now be scrambling to fill in the gaps. There were some follow-up calls to make, but after that it would be back to the drudgery of cold calling to set up leads for presentations and interviews. Now in his late thirties, he had hoped his career had surpassed that level but the death of Schneider changed everything.

Kay had resumed her role as homemaker in his life, puttering around the house and finding things to tidy and sort out. Her tight jeans did a lot to restore some of his exuberance, and he was very happy to have her back as a daily companion. They had not discussed the option of her moving back in, but he was sure that after a few romantic interludes, it would be an unspoken progression.

"Max, are you going to go out and shovel oats for Edd?" she called in as she prepared breakfast that morning. "I can see he's a big eater, he's pretty well at the bottom of the feeder."

"I just filled that up yesterday," Max looked up from the *San Antonio Express-News*, which he got regularly along with the *Austin American Statesman* as a result of being nearly equidistant from both major cities. "I checked with the Board of Health a little while ago and they said that the lab reports should be back by noon. Hopefully I'll be able to get Edd back to the stables where I've got those big mangers."

"I must say, you did a wonderful job grooming him," Kay praised him. "I told you he was white, not gray. He's so Bridgman now he almost has a silver sheen. He must have been badly undernourished. He looks like a different horse now."

"I—I haven't been out there," Max managed. He had gone out to the garage shortly after calling Kay, realizing that it was there that he received the premonition about Dennis. Edd was standing at rest, and once again Max began questioning his own faculties as there was no more communication from the horse. He made a subconscious decision to avoid the garage until he could get his head together. He spent most of the day watching the Austin newscasts trying to find out more about Dennis' death, and sifting through his prospective clientele files. Kay spent most of the day and left that evening before Max dropped off into a fitful sleep.

"Well, I hope you're not feeling guilty about Sugar and projecting it on Edd," she came over and patted his shoulder as he sat at his desk in his office. "Maybe you can send him off to another stable for the time being until you get things back in order around here."

"No, no, that's fine," he kissed her hand. He realized that they had not been this romantic in quite a while, and it was doing him a world of good as he had been starving for it. Only it could not have come at a more inopportune time, and his biggest fear was that she might mistake it for disinterest and fly the coop again. "I'll go out there and see him now. Say, are you gonna go up with me to Dennis' wake tomorrow?"

"I can if you want me to."

"Why wouldn't I want to be seen with the sexiest girl in town?"

"Well, maybe you'd rather be with the prettiest, or the smartest."

"Come here, you," he grabbed her wrist and pulled her into his lap. "You're all three of them rolled into one, you know that."

"Well, I don't mind you reminding me," she smiled sweetly. They exchanged loving kisses before she wriggled free.

"I know where this is going to end up, and I've got some vacuuming to do before I head off to see Mother," she smoothed her red plaid flannel shirt. "I'll be back to fix supper, and I'll bring my black dress so I can spend the night if we're leaving in the morning."

"Don't forget your negligee and those thigh highs."

"You're incorrigible," she chuckled as she headed back to the kitchen.

He decided to take a break from sorting out his hot leads in his file box, always having been a bit old-fashioned in keeping his leads on index cards rather than recording them electronically. He always felt more comfortable in having the leads literally at his fingertips rather than on Excel or MS Word where they might be erased or lost in a crash. He got up and stretched, then slipped on his cowboy boots and went out the sliding glass door, climbing over the short iron railing and heading to the garage.

The sight of the horse standing in front of the garage was almost distracting. He seemed taller and heavier, and had indeed become a shade lighter. Max was almost startled into thinking that someone had come in and switched horses on him. Things had gotten so crazy around here that he could not have been accused of being paranoid by wondering if the Government was testing some mind-control device on him, escalating the fear factor by planting the anthrax and having his political client assassinated.

"What's going on with you, Wonder Horse?" Max came over and hugged his face before marveling at his shiny white hide. "Are you part cat, have you learned to lick yourself clean? You know, I wouldn't have put it past Kay to have brushed you down and ribbed me for it. Anyway, you look great, fellow. Plus, I owe you for that tip on Dennis. I'll be sure and ask Kay to pick up a bag of apples and some carrots on her way back from town."

Just then a gust of wind blew in from the hills, knocking a straw basket of wildflowers Kay had picked off a table by the garage. Max went over and replaced the flowers before putting the basket back on the table.

Don't mention it.

"Nope, no way," Max held his hands to his head, laughing at himself. "No way."

With that he headed back to the house, going back to the task of filling the void in his life left by Dennis Schneider.

The health inspector called about an hour later and told Max that the tests had come back negative. He decided he would wait until they came back from Austin before giving the stables a good scrubbing so as to move Edd to his new residence. He spent the day sorting out leads and making follow-up calls before narrowing down the field to four prospects. There were two candidates running for office in San Antonio, a candidate in Austin and one in Waco. He felt as if Waco would be taking a step backward, and San Antonio would be a bit laid back for him. Austin was where the action was in the seat of power, and he was going to hit up Senator Bill Goldsworthy as soon as he got back into town.

Goldsworthy was a conservative Christian running on a platform that seemed conducive to Republicans, the Tea Party and the reactionaries alike. He promised a return to traditional Christian American values and the restoration of the prestige of American society and its culture. The word on the Internet was that the Administration was alarmed by Goldworthy's meteoric rise on the Southwest political scene and was furiously digging to find a blemish on his impeccable reputation. The man that the right-wing coalition was now calling the Mediator seemed unstoppable at this juncture.

Max called and left a detailed message upon being sent to voicemail. He mentioned meeting Goldsworthy at a political rally last fall and that they had exchanged business cards. He informed him that his previous commitment to Dennis Schneider had ended tragically and that he was interested in discussing the possibility of contributing to Goldsworthy's campaign. He left his phone number, cell number, e-mail address and Kay's cell number. If he could cut a deal with Goldsworthy, he was certain that his career would continue to skyrocket past the Schneider campaign.

Kay returned from her mother's as planned, and she made a sumptuous sirloin steak dinner with creamed broccoli and baked potatoes along with her mint-flavored iced tea. She even brought a bag of Granny Smith apples for Max to share with Edd, and a sackful of carrots. Kay had never been much of a horse person even though she was a skilled rider, and had never spent as much time with Sugar as she did with Edd. Max considered the fact that, in the turbulence of their previous relationship, she might have subconsciously thought of Sugar as some sort of rival for his affections. He took pleasure in the notion that her warm embrace was now big enough for a husband and a horse.

They woke up before sunrise the following morning after an evening of glorious lovemaking (she had indeed brought her negligee and black nylons), and she prepared a king's breakfast before they dressed in black business wear for Schneider's wake. He had gotten a call from Bill Goldsworthy's office, informing him that the Senator was out of town but would be delighted to meet with him this weekend. Kay was excited for him, and they spent most of the ride to Austin speculating on the opportunities awaiting should he strike a deal with Goldsworthy.

Just before they took off, Max went out to the stable to check on Edd's water and bring him an apple and a carrot. He refrained from bringing out the sugar cubes that he used to give Sugar (which is how she got her name) because Kay always chided him for giving her unhealthy processed food. Still, he was sure that Edd would love the fruit and vegetable, and hopefully he would saddle him up and take him for a ride this weekend.

Max decided to measure Edd because he was strongly suspecting his imagination was carrying him away. He knew how pet owners always wanted to have the biggest and strongest animal on the block, and were constantly checking to see if their kitten had grown an inch or their puppy gained a pound. In this case, his mind was tricking him into thinking Edd was growing daily, though Dr. Altchek assured him that the horse was at least five years old. Although a horse reached maturity at three, its spine continued to grow until its fifth year. Even so, daily growth was a physical impossibility, even if Max had loaded him up with a truckful of steroids. Max measured him three times at ten hands high, and wrote the number in ballpoint on his writs before heading back to the house.

Check out the man with the gray suit.

"What?" Max stopped short, the voice in his head startling him.

The man with the gray suit.

Max whirled and stared at Edd as he took a drink of water, then turned and stared straight into his eyes.

"Are you talking to me again?"

Edd blinked before turning to his feeder.

"Come on, boy, you're scaring the crap out of me," Max went over and stroked his neck "What man? What gray suit?"

Edd raised his head up and down in a nodding motion before returning to his oats.

Max knew that he was going to resolve this issue in very short order, but knew not where to start. He had to tell someone, but he knew if he mentioned this to Kay, she would demand that he make an appointment with a psychiatrist. He also realized that if he spoke to his doctor about it, he would probably make the same suggestion. All roads led to the loony bin, but Max was sure that there was far more to it.

He could not help but think that perhaps his contact with Goldsworthy had exacerbated the situation. If the Administration had targeted Goldsworthy as a threat to their quasi-socialist regime, then in all likelihood they would be looking at Max as well. If things kept going in this direction, then the anthrax contamination and the killing of Schneider, along with these mind control attempts, was some kind of segue towards a meeting with some man in a gray suit.

At once he felt like kicking himself for his paranoid stupidity. He knew if there were any such thing as mind controlling brain scanners, they would have been put to use in taking down the Iranians and the North Koreans long before getting around to Max Bridgman. He promised himself to research this disembodied voice phenomenon as soon as he got back from Austin.

Gray suit.

"Aah, bullshit," Max waved at Edd before returning to the house to escort Kay to the car.

They arrived at the funeral home where the family members were being vastly outnumbered by political supporters coming out to mourn the unbelievable loss of one of their rising stars. A significant number of media people had also come out for comments and opinions on what lay ahead for the dysfunctional conservative movement in the Lone Star State.

"Oh, Max," Sylvia Schneider rose from her front-row seat in front of the massive coffin to exchange embraces with him as he came over. He introduced her to Kay, and the women hugged each other before the mature yet attractive woman turned to Max.

"This is just terrible, it's like a nightmare," she wept. "I'll be sure and have our accountant settle up any outstanding payments with you. I just don't know where to start, I can't believe that something like this could have happened."

"Excuse me, Mr. Bridgman," one of Dennis' assistant campaign managers came by as newcomers made their way over to Mrs. Schneider. "There's a gentleman who would like to speak with you. Dennis called him just before the accident occurred. He had wanted to schedule a meeting between the three of you. The gentleman would still like to have a word."

"I'll be in the back," Kay touched his arm reassuringly, nodding to a couple of empty seats in the far corner of the parlor. Max kissed her cheek before following the manager.

Max was introduced to a tall, powerfully-built man wearing mirrored sunglasses and an expensive gray designer suit. Schneider's rep announced the man as Cory Roper before taking his leave.

"Mr. Bridgman, I'm a representative of the WCS here in Austin," Roper was diplomatic. "We had been discussing a number of pertinent issues with Mr. Schneider before his untimely demise, and it seems that we had reached an agreement on a number of key points. Now, as you know, his departure has left a void along the horizon. All of us who are part of the conservative coalition here in Austin want to see our network repaired as soon as possible."

"How can I help?" Max wondered.

"Word around the campfire is that Senator Bill Goldsworthy has been mentioning your name as a possible addition to his campaign office. Our district leaders at WCS feel that Mr. Goldsworthy is a very capable man and, quite honestly, a shining light that can guide our next generation to a promising future. As you know, the immigration issue is a deep-rooted problem in this country. Illegal aliens are overburdening our social services system and facilitating the entry of terrorists across our borders. Confounding the situation is this knee-jerk reaction by the Government using the infiltration as an excuse to monitor the Internet and violate our Constitutional rights."

"I can assure you that Mr. Schneider had expressed grave concerns about these issues," Max assured him. "I agree that someone is going to have to fill the gap Dennis left behind, and Bill Goldsworthy may very well be the man. Personally, I don't even have my foot in the door yet, and I'd be misleading you to make you think I could do anything to help your cause at this point."

"Our cause is the preventive maintenance of this great nation," Roper was emphatic. "I know you see things our way, and you can count on our support."

As Roper departed, Max involuntarily shuddered at the thought of bringing the WCS to the table as part of his negotiations with Goldsworthy. This was going to require a great deal of thought, and his only hope was that some fantastic Government mind control project would not become a factor in the equation.

Chapter Fourteen

Max and Kay returned to New Braunfels that night and cuddled in each others' arms as they were soon fast asleep after the considerable drive home. They were invited back to the Schneiders' spacious home in Round Rock where they were introduced to a large number of people they would most likely never meet again. They all reminisced over the accomplishments of Dennis Schneider, and lamented the great loss to the community caused by his untimely death. The continued commiseration proved to be emotionally exhausting over a couple of hours' time, and the Bridgmans were glad to be relieved of it when the Schneider clan finally called it a night.

When Max awoke the next morning, he got a call from Cory Roper advising him that one of his representatives would be making appearances in San Antonio that evening and was hoping to meet with him. Max was reluctant but Roper insisted that Larry Clarkson had an engagement at UTSA and would be able to meet him near the campus for lunch. Max had not been out to visit his old alma mater in over a year, and finally relented. He was given Clarkson's cell number and agreed he would call about 11 AM when he reached Loop 1604.

"I hope you're planning to keep a safe distance from these people," Kay admonished him as he prepared for his drive after breakfast. Kay was politically astute and kept abreast of local, national and world events on the Internet on a daily basis. She was a graduate of St. Mary's University with a teaching degree but, after having married Max, never was forced to pursue her vocation. Max had no problem discussing politics with Kay and rarely felt as if she was talking off the top of her head. "You don't want to lose sight of the fact that these people are extremists by nature. If you start getting associated with them, it could wreck your own political future."

At once he flashed back to his last conversation with Dennis when they set up the meeting that was cancelled by his fatal accident. He remembered Dennis mentioning the WCS when he told him about the anthrax that killed Sugar. What made him discount the WCS as suspects if, in fact, someone had contaminated the stable with the virus? He was so distraught that it had not even crossed his mind until now. Was Dennis aware that the WCS might still be targeting actual or suspected political rivals or enemies? If so, why would they have possibly considered a move on Max unless they were already zeroing in on Dennis? Maybe Dennis' request was not so much to coordinate efforts with WCS as an attempt at reconciliation. Suddenly things seemed more ominous than he had perceived at face value.

"Kay, could I ask you a favor?" he said softly. "You know I don't like to impose on you to get caught up in my business, but I'm just getting bombarded here and I'd hate to get caught short unnecessarily."

"Okay, dollface, what do you have?" she stood with hands on hips. They had tried to have her do his secretarial work years ago, and the project failed miserably. She just did not have the time or patience to do the research that Max was particularly adept at.

"I'd like to start a little file on WCS," he decided. "Who they've targeted over the last few years, where they turned the corner as to their political strategy, and if they've actually gone mainstream or are just obfuscating their agenda. I'd like to know who's trying to drag me into bed besides my lovely wife."

"You certainly have a way with words," she shook her head. "Okay, one scoopful of dirt on WCS coming up."

Now the paranoia was really kicking in as he considered whether WCS had been trying to coerce Dennis into stepping onto their platform, or vice versa. Even worse, had they possibly set up the hit-and-run attack on Dennis, waiting to see if he would leave the house during the late evening on an emergency run to the pharmacy? He knew that pain was almost impossible to measure from one individual to another, and migraines could be one of the most dreaded sources. If Sylvia Schneider had been chugging down the hydrocodone during a particularly vicious episode, Dennis could easily have rushed out to the car in a moment's notice after phoning the on-call pharmacist. If anyone had been spying on him, they could well have anticipated the drug run and set him up for the fatal collision.

There was a police bulletin on the news since the incident giving details about the event, asking any witnesses to come forward in an attempt to apprehend the hit-and-run driver. No one had responded, and it was well known that murder cases usually ran cold after twenty-four hours. If, in fact, WCS had anything to do with it, they might be trying to consolidate the fruits of their labor by using Max to get to Bill Goldsworthy. Not only would he be wanting to do all he could to protect Goldsworthy, but he would also be wanting to uncover any plot that might have existed to eliminate Dennis Schneider.

His mind began to reel with the thought of Dennis having been assassinated, and Goldsworthy possibly being next on the list. It made him sick to think that he might be getting inextricably entwined in this plot. Most certainly someone would want to find out exactly what Dennis' last conversation with Max was about, and for good reason. Dennis did indeed bring WCS up in that discussion, and Max was now obsessed with discovering why. Certainly whoever might have had something to do with killing Dennis would want to know the same thing.

He heard Kay logging in on the computer, and then into their Internet account. He hoped she did not start digging into her e-mail first, but he would not even go there. He decided that if she got sidetracked, he would just do a quick Google search and take that with him to his meeting with Clarkson at UTSA. Dennis had no misconceptions about these people, and neither would Max unless Kay came across substantiating evidence indicating they had taken a major philosophical turn somewhere.

It was entirely possible that they might have channeled their xenophobia onto the illegal immigration platform. There was more than one way to promote their race hatred agenda from within. Dallas was a perfect example, and so was Selma and Schertz right down the road. Illegals driving through those towns were as likely as not to be dealing with Border Patrol once they got hauled in by the local police's racial profiling patrol. WCS' best move was to gain the mainstream acceptance they needed to get some political leverage, and hitching their wagon to a rising star would be the best way to get it done.

Max decided to lie down on the couch until Kay got done with her research. He was not one for extensive driving over a stretch of time, and was not looking forward to a cruise to San Antonio after having just gotten back from Round Rock last night. Kay did not like sitting in the passenger's seat for long periods either, so she would be sympathetic. He would plan on meeting her back here for supper, and hopefully he would be gearing up for his meeting with Goldsworthy once he cleared his slate.

"Okay, Romeo," Kay roused him from his nap about an hour later. "Here's your poop. There's a few news items about them becoming a kinder, gentler conehead group. Now they're all about the preservation of white Christian America rather than racial purity and ethnic cleansing. All of their websites and online groups are on about that Christian Identity malarkey, the stuff about the Jews and other minorities having evolved from the Devil. Don't be looking forward to a deep intellectual conversation with this fellow."

"Thanks, darling," he took the folder and kissed her hand as he sat up and yawned. "I guess I'll go ahead and get ready, I'll leave in about an hour. It should take about a half hour to get to the campus by eleven with traffic."

"You know, I figured I'd go ahead and take Edd for a short run," she decided. "He's been sitting out there by himself for the last couple of days, and god knows how long he was left out at that vacant house. He's really a beautiful horse, and it's a shame how someone would just abandon him like that."

"That sounds like a great idea," he replied. "You know where I keep my saddle. I never did call the Sheriff to find out about that house where I found him. Then again, maybe I should leave well enough alone so that no one turns up to take him back."

"I'll probably come back and shower up before I head out to Mother's. You'll probably be gone by then, so I'll see you at supper." She leaned over and kissed him, then headed off to the stable.

"Say, wait up and I'll go out with you," he decided, jogging over and slipping out the patio door behind her. She held his hand as they walked over to the stable, and he saddled Edd for her before they trotted off.

Say goodbye.

"What?" he inadvertently called after them.

"What what?" she smiled back.

"I thought you said something," he shrugged. "See you in a bit."

He headed back to the couch and idly flipped through the file and the copies Kay made. It was just as Kay said, mostly rants about white supremacy and the Jews orchestrating the pollution of Caucasian blood. He could easily see how these people weren't going to make it to first base without a major push from someone. He found it odd that these groups were the only ones who couldn't find their place in mainstream politics. Race-oriented groups were making impacts across the country among minorities, and even street gangs were making their voices heard in major cities throughout the nation. If these guys just quit dragging their knuckles and bellowing their rhetoric at every opportunity, they might at least gain a foothold somewhere.

He took his time shaving and showering, leisurely getting dressed as the clock ticked on. He figured he would take a stroll around the campus before or after his meeting with Clarkson and see how much things changed since last year. Maybe he'd see one of his professors. He was sure they would be glad to see that one of their former students had moved up in the world. Even though he was not much for e-mail correspondence, he would try and get some addys and do his best to keep in touch.

It was about 10:15, and he decided to check on Kay and Edd before taking off. He had a pair of binoculars hanging by the door so he could look over the field whenever he wanted without having to ride, drive or walk across the grassy plain. He grabbed them off the hook and stepped out onto the patio, scanning the area to see where they went.

He saw a couple of objects on the ground in the distance, and adjusted the focus to get a clear view. He gasped in horror as he realized it was Kay and Edd, both of them lying prone in the dust. He turned and hung the binoculars back on the hook and began racing wildly from the patio, onto the field and across the plain to where they had fallen.

The sun was coming up and it was probably close to ninety degrees by now. Max had not gotten in much exercise as of late, and this was probably a 200-yard dash to where they were. He knew Kay was an experienced rider, and riding horses was a lot like riding bikes. Once one learned, they were not likely to forget and took little time to shake the rust off. Most likely they had hit a gopher hole that Max had been unaware of and had not been able to come out and refill. If neither of them were able to regain their feet, he would have to call the sheriff and an ambulance. He had forgotten to grab his cell phone but was sure Kay had hers.

He was gasping for breath by the time he reached them, and he was shocked by what he found. Kay's head was crooked at a frightening angle, and her eyes were widened as if going into shock. Edd was writhing and snorting, a huge piece of bone protruding from his left shin. Max looked about in a daze and saw a small hole, probably dug by a groundhog, that was well covered by surrounding sagebrush. If Kay had Edd in a gallop, she probably never saw it in time.

"Max?" her voice was almost a whisper.

"Kay, baby," tears came to his eyes, realizing she might have broken her neck. "Don't you move. Do you have your cell phone? I'll call the Sheriff."

"In my—pocket—"

He gently pushed his hand into her pocket and pulled out her phone. To his dismay, he could not get a signal.

"It's not working," he jumped to his feet. "Let me run back to the house, I'll call the sheriff and bring the car up. Hold tight, sweetheart."

He ran back with all the energy he had left, and he was drenched in sweat by the time he had gotten within twenty yards of the house. He was running in such a state of exhaustion that his legs were flailing mechanically, and he had little control as he tripped over a rock and sprained his ankle. The pain was agonizing, and he was unable to put enough weight on it to get back to his feet. He was forced to crawl over the last twenty yards, through the patio door and over to the kitchen counter where he kept a land line.

He dialed 911, and was barely able to give the operator the information she impatiently demanded before the combined shock and heat exhaustion swept him into unconsciousness.

* * *

"He's coming around."

Max could hear voices and groggily opened his eyes, trying to focus and figure out where he was. He seemed to be in a dimly lit room and realized he was in a hospital. He looked around and saw a male nurse standing alongside a deputy sheriff.

"He'll be okay," the nurse told the deputy. "I'll be right outside, call me if you need me."

"Mr. Bridgman? I'm Deputy Young with the Sheriff's Department. You're in Christus Santa Rosa. We brought you here as soon as the ambulance arrived. Fortunately you gave us all the information we needed and we were able to locate your wife and the horse."

"How is she? Where's Kay?"

"I'm sorry, Mr. Bridgman, but your wife did not survive her injuries. We contacted your mother-in-law, and she is attending to the situation as we speak.

We brought your horse back to the stable, and secured your house as best we could. The doctor indicated that you should be able to go home."

"No," Max dissolved into tears. "Not Kay. Oh god, no."

"Has she ever rode a horse like that before?" the deputy asked quietly.

"She's rode horses all her life," Max tried to control his voice.

"I'm terribly sorry for your loss, Mr. Bridgman," the deputy said softly before taking his leave. "You can call the Sheriff's Office if you have any questions or need additional information."

The nurse returned and told Max that he had a badly sprained ankle, and would probably need crutches that would be made available at the front desk. Max was insured by Humana and the policy covered most of the cost outside of a moderate copay. He dressed with some difficulty and was taken by wheelchair to the lobby where he was given crutches and some hydrocodone as they processed the insurance claim. He was then wheeled out to the emergency exit where a cab had been summoned to take him home.

The drive back was largely a blur as he tried to piece it all together. He was sickened by the thought of Kay having been killed in the accident. He was filled with remorse but could not possibly blame himself. The notion of stopping her from riding Edd would have caused an outrage. She had been riding most of her life, and such a suggestion would have appeared as if he had some weird reason behind it. There was no way that asking her not to ride Edd would have ever crossed his mind.

He directed the cabbie to let him off by the stable, where he would come to grips with the miracle that allowed the deputies to have brought Edd back home. He knew enough about horses to have fully expected Edd to have been put to sleep by an animal control officer as a humane act of mercy. His shin had been horribly broken, and unless the Government had developed some fantastic new technique to restore horses' legs, someone somewhere had truly worked a miracle.

He nearly dropped his cane in shock as he switched on the light in the stable and beheld a gigantic Clydesdale, the biggest horse he had ever seen. It was a silvery white, its magnificent mane, tail and hoof hair shimmering in the dimness.

Just you and me.

Chapter Fifteen

Max Bridgman was at once overwhelmed by a paroxysm of anger towards this horse. The animal's arrival into his life presaged the demise of Sugar, the killing of Dennis Schneider and now the death of Kay. Maybe the Government was using some sort of mind-control technique to manipulate his brain waves, but there was no way in hell they could have turned this little plug into a Clydesdale. Obviously they switched horses on him, and now they had crossed the line by killing Kay. He would come back at them with everything he had, and someone somewhere was going to regret the fact they had picked the wrong target. *Check my foreleg.*

"Look, you," Max popped up from the feeder upon which he had been sitting. "Stick it up your ass! I know you can't talk, and for those government bastards who're using you as a prop, they're gonna rue the day they ever thought of screwing with Max Bridgman!"

Foreleg.

Max mechanically stumbled over to Edd, his ankle still smarting though the hydrocodone nearly had him in La-La Land. He bent over to check his left leg and nearly fell over in shock as he saw a deep scar exactly where Max had seen bone protruding hours ago. He recovered himself and felt the leg, detecting a large crevice in the bone as if it had been a once-fractured human limb badly reset.

"How?" Max nearly fell back on his butt, and had to crawl back now that his ankle was catching fire anew. "How are you doing this? Why?"

Goldsworthy.

"No," Max gasped. "You can't, you son of a bitch!"

He reeled backwards into the feeder, then reflexively grabbed his crutches and headed back to the house. He knew that if he tarried, his ankle would start screaming bloody murder and he might not make it afterwards. He contemplated sending the beast to a glue factory, or some horsemeat processor in New Jersey. He could even work up a storyline after coming back with his pistol and shooting the bastard. Yet he eventually came to realize that the horse was just a prop being used by the Government to make him think he was going crazy. They probably even worked the Clydesdale's leg to make it look like the gray (off-white?) horse's leg had healed as it morphed into a magnificent steed.

He unlocked the door and switched on the light, hobbling into his comfortably-furnished living room with the great sliding doors facing the prairie at the foot of the Central Texas hills. They might well have been out there, spies from Homeland Security or even the CIA, zeroing in on him with their mind-control device, trying to throw him on a collision course with Bill Goldsworthy next. He yanked off his shirt and tie, trying to sort out what they were trying to do to him before planning a course of action.

It seemed as if they were trying to eliminate all of their right-wing opposition, and were wedging in the WCS as a safety catch to refocus blame if one of their schemes went wrong. Turning Max into a raving loony running around warning everyone of the Government's mind control plot would be proof positive that the inmates were running the Conservative asylum.

He was trying to piece together what had happened and what they might've done. Killing Sugar could have easily been a low-level anthrax attack, and alerting him to what happened to Dennis was what had triggered the whole scam to make him believe Edd was clairvoyant and had telepathic abilities, not to mention human intelligence. Giving him a heads-up on Cory Roper would establish the link to WCS. But why in hell did they have to kill Kay?

It dawned on him that he had forgotten all about calling Larry Clarkson. He also hadn't spoken to Darlene Aniston yet. He hobbled over to the kitchen counter and got on the phone, finding his voicemail was full. The first call he made was to Clarkson, who was nettled at first, then deeply apologetic when he learned the reason for Max's no-call no-show.

"I truly am sorry, Max," Larry said apologetically with a deep Southern accent. "On behalf of WCS I wish to convey my condolences as well as those of the organization. If there's anything at all we can do, just call me or Cory Roper."

Sure, Max thought. How about a good old cross-burning at the funeral? Maybe we can get a conehead color guard going, with some Confederate flags and WCS banners.

"I certainly do appreciate it, Larry. I'll give you a call when I drive up to Austin to meet Bill Goldsworthy. Maybe we can meet up when I get back to town."

Why not, he figured after hanging up. He had no one to come home to now that Kay was gone. All his family and relatives were up in Chicago, and he had made few connections at UTSA, largely considered a transit campus. The only one left was Darlene, and when he called her he got sent to voicemail. He left a message that he was devastated by the tragedy and that he would be coming out to see her as soon as he heard from her. Chances were that she probably never wanted to see him again after having been unable to prevent her daughter's death.

He decided to wait until morning to try and reach Goldsworthy, and wondered if that was going to happen for him. He knew that Edd's mind manipulators had mentioned the Senator, and he couldn't help but think that perhaps they were going to make an attempt on his life. If he tried to warn Goldsworthy, he would be seen as a crackpot and dismissed once and forever. His only chance was to confirm their meeting this weekend and gain his confidence in order to help prevent a possible assassination.

Just before he decided to pack it in for the night, he got a call on the phone. He was going to let it go to voicemail but quickly answered when he saw Goldsworthy's name on Caller ID.

"Max, this is Bill Goldsworthy," he spoke in a Texas drawl.

"I just got back into town and got the message from the office. I'm going to be here for a political rally Saturday night and I was hoping we could meet up then."

"That'd be swell, Senator," Max managed, his mind swirling with thoughts of Kay's funeral arrangements. If they picked out a funeral home by tomorrow, they'd probably have the wake by Thursday at the latest. If the burial was Sunday he had plenty of time to get back, but missing the service Saturday night would haunt him for the rest of his days. "If you can e-mail me the particulars I'll look forward to meeting you there."

After they hung up, Max's stomach was churning with tension. He knew that this would probably sever all ties with Kay's family forever after this, but the thought of risking Goldsworthy's life in an assassination plot was out of the question. He had to attend the rally and make the connection with Goldsworthy, then do everything in his power to earn the man's trust in order to warn him of what might very well lie ahead.

Max woke up the next morning and drove out to Darlene's to help her get everything sorted out. Her two sons lived out of state and would be arriving with their families Thursday morning. Max found himself handling everything for Darlene as she was totally distracted by the tragedy. Fortunately he had kept Kay on all his policies, which covered everything from the funeral to the burial with the life insurance payment. It would turn into a reimbursement, but fortunately Max had enough squirreled away to bear the brunt of the upfront costs.

It had been an exhausting day, and he was going to call it a night by 7 PM when the phone rang. He picked it up without looking at the caller ID and found it was Cory Roper. He called to inquire if he had any contact with Bill Goldsworthy's office about the rally scheduled in Austin this Saturday. Max told him he had already planned to meet with Goldsworthy at the event, and Roper told him that Larry Clarkson would be there with a couple of WCS representatives as well.

"Things are happening quick, Max," Roper was enthusiastic. "We took a hard body shot by losing Dennis, but I do believe that the Good Lord provides." *Well, I hope He'll provide something for me before it's too late,* Max thought to himself after hanging up.

Going to the funeral home was the worst part of the day, probably the worst episode of his life. They allowed him down to the basement to see Kay, and she appeared as if sleeping with a look of serenity on her face. Yet she had that mannequin look as a semblance of herself, the life gone and just the beautiful shell remaining. He sobbed in silence, keeping his pain to himself as best he could as he placed his hands over hers, as marble beneath the white silk gloves. It convinced him that she was truly gone, and all he could hope was that he would be worthy of joining her in the Heaven where he was sure she awaited.

Having to explain his absence at the Saturday night rosary was the absolute worst of all, the straw that broke the camel's back as far as all were concerned. He explained the situation to Darlene, who said nothing but had the look in her eye that reminded him that it was in his company where she lost her daughter, on his property, as an estranged husband who never deserved her. Her brothers were somewhat more sympathetic but still could not see how a business meeting could not have been postponed. Their families said goodbye, but their subdued manners said everything that Darlene did not.

He drove up to Austin in a world of hurt, and reached the Senator's office shortly before five PM. Bill Goldsworthy was a tall, graying man with an athletic build and a strong personality. He immediately expressed his condolences and gratitude for Max coming out at such a difficult time, and suggested they stop for coffee and some time to talk before they headed off to the rally scheduled for 8 PM.

They stopped at Ruta Maya near Sixth Street in Austin, the bohemian coffee house providing them with a comfortable place to relax with its overstuffed chairs and lounge tables situated in a side room adjoining the warehouse-size restaurant area. College kids and local artists loved the place, and Goldsworthy was never surprised to see his political colleagues there from time to time.

"Senator, I've been greatly concerned about the conspiracy theories that have been circulating over the past few months," Max came right to the point after they exchanged pleasantries about the weather and the coffee house ambiance. "I haven't gotten comfortable with the fact that Dennis' death remains an unsolved hit-and-run case. I've also got reason to believe the government may be directing clandestine activities against political opponents here in Central Texas. I don't have any proof as yet, but my life's been tossed upside down over the past week and I can't believe it's all a matter of circumstance."

"Do you feel like you're being targeted?"

"I don't think it's just me," Max leaned forward intently. "I think they might have been looking at Dennis, and I think they may be making a series of preemptive moves against those who they think is blocking their socialist agenda."

"Well, I think we're all aware that there may be turbulent times ahead," Goldsworthy steepled his fingers. "I don't mean to pry, but, are you a Christian?"

"My wife and I are—were—uh, Catholics," he fumbled about. "We go—uh, went to church together on the holidays. She wasn't much of a church person, sorry to say."

"I don't want you to get the wrong impression, or feel as if I'm trying to sway you in any way, but many of those of us on the conservative side are born-again evangelical Christians. There are a large number of us who believe there are dark days ahead for those of the faith. We don't think it's something we can avoid, but it certainly helps to try and understand."

"So do you think it's the government targeting Christians, people of faith?"

"Well, in the Epistles, the apostle Paul speaks of our conflict against the powers and principalities in high places, the forces of darkness. We recognize the fact that the Devil is the god of this world, and that he holds sway over those in authority. We can only do our best to intercede as best we can and to alleviate the injustices brought against our people."

"So you're looking past the government conspiracy, you're seeing it as a supernatural phenomena," Max tried to summarize.

"Precisely. We are like the little Dutch boy with his finger in the dike. Hopefully enough of our people will be able to reach shelter before the dam explodes." Max allowed the conversation to drift off in other directions until it was time for them to head out for the rally. It was being held at the Stephen F. Austin Hotel on Congress Avenue, and the streets were lined with limousines as dozens of political luminaries were making the scene. They took the short walk up to the hotel and exchanged handshakes with attendees who knew Goldsworthy, as well as Max by his association with Dennis Schneider.

The notion of this being some kind of supernatural conspiracy made Max queasier than ever. These people were way beyond political conspiracies; this was something you couldn't even discuss with someone outside the loop. How was he going to convince anyone that he had been targeted by the Devil, who was masterminding a plot to drive him crazy with a mind control technique? This was getting worse and worse, and the only thing he could imagine that could work in his favor was that this surfaced in the media and that he could step forth and declare himself a victim. Whatever the case may be, it sure would make it a lot easier for everyone involved if they could all sit back and say the Devil made them do it.

They had reservations at a table not far from the dais at the front of the banquet hall, and immediately the flow of well-wishers began as Goldsworthy arrived at his seat. Max noticed that Larry Clarkson was seated at a table across the aisle from them, and he came over and shook hands as a number of what he perceived as WCS goons arrived at the table.

Man in the black suit.

Max was shocked by the mental impulse, as if Edd was right here in the room with him. He stared around frantically, looking for men in black suits which abounded throughout the room, as well as searching for signs of Edd himself. He suddenly caught sight of a man in black rising from the WCS table, carrying a gun straight towards the aisle towards Goldsworthy's table. Max was overwhelmed by an adrenalin rush, hurling himself straight at the WCS man. He slammed into the man, and guests at nearby tables saw what was happening and began piling on the fallen gunman.

"Let me go, you sons of bitches!" the WCS man screamed and cursed. "Stop that guy!"

Max whirled again and saw yet another man in a black suit emerging from the crowd of newcomers, raising a pistol in Bill Goldsworthy's direction. He made another frenzied rush as the Senator recoiled, raising his arms to block the shot. The assassin fired, hitting Goldsworthy right between the eyes. Max dove through the air to block the automatic volley, and one of the bullets caught him in the chest and lodged in his heart.

He was driven directly to the University Medical Center and underwent emergency surgery but they were unable to save him. His relatives in Chicago were notified and they were able to make all the necessary arrangements. About a week later, Max and Kay Bridgman were resting in peace together in their family plot which remained unused less than a month ago.

Shortly after Max was laid to rest, Corey Roper made inquiries as to Bridgman's estate and found that his mother-in-law Darlene had stepped forth to handle things on behalf of the extended family. Larry Clarkson contacted Darlene and told her he was interested in taking the property off her hands, and they quickly went about settling the matter. WCS was hoping that Darlene would leave most of Max's paperwork untouched, and as it turned out, all she had the moving company reclaim was his furniture, fixtures and personal items. Clarkson readily offered to dispose of all the papers and files lying about.

Clarkson's daughter Eva came out to see their new ranch home and was delighted by the beauty of the surrounding area. She loved animals and was thrilled to find out that there was a stable out back of the house. The teenager went out to investigate and rushed over to where she saw the smallish, off-white horse alone in the stable.

"Hi there, cutie!" she joyfully patted the horse's face. "I'm Eva! I wonder what they call you."

At once there was a still, small voice, and she was certain that the hill country wind was playing tricks with her imagination.

My name is Edd.